NOTHING
BEAT

SCARLETT FINN

ISBN: 9781917248402

www.scarlettfinn.com

Also by Scarlett Finn

ONE

"COME ON, LADIES! This is the premium Breckenridge steed, this generation's original model! You get twenty-four hours of this bachelor's time. Very valuable time. Doesn't have to be consecutive hours, you can spread him out any way you like." Ha, subtle. "This is a great lot, ladies! A valuable prize for a lucky bidder... We've got to start the bidding at fifty! Who'll give me fifty?" The auctioneer pointed out to the side. "Thank you, ma'am." He clapped once. "Oh, and, Alice, I got word from Mr. Breckenridge Senior, he doesn't want you paying to bring your sons home, they cost him enough already."

Ah, funny, and the room responded in kind.

"Sixty!" someone shouted.

"A hundred!"

Bidding on the Breckenridge bachelor continued. The auctioneer at the podium on stage fielded the speed and urgency of pledges.

Beautiful ballroom, glamorous gowns, the festive event was dedicated to charity, raising money for those in need. Wonderful cause. Just so happened, she too was in need, though it wasn't of cash.

Breck, said bachelor being bid on, would be reaching the edge of his patience. Theater wasn't his thing, even if his gorgeous face was fit for stage or screen. Was she biased? Yes. But anyone who denied his hotness would be flat out lying. No wonder he was a popular lot.

Time to put an end to the competition.

Rising, she lifted a hand to call out over all the others. "One million dollars!"

A collective gasp prompted a round of applause. She'd never been applauded before, not that she could remember. Being far at the back of the room, she couldn't decipher the twitch of Breck's curious eyelid; good thing she didn't need to see to know it was there.

"I think we have a winner, ladies and gentlemen! Come on up and claim your prize, ma'am. Congratulations!"

Gliding away from the table, she wound around the others and ascended the stairs at the side of the stage. Did she want to go up there in front of everyone? Everyone who? Before she'd raised her eyes from the final stair, Breck's hand had already appeared in her line of sight, open for hers. Under his spotlight, they were completely alone, not just in the room, but on the planet.

Oh, Rankin Breckenridge, better known as just 'Breck' was nothing if not predictable.

She took his proffered hand, of course—any excuse to touch him—and waved to the masses as he led her backstage. The auctioneer was quick to move onto the next lot.

Good, that was them, forgotten. On to the next stage of her plan.

"Coy, what are you doing?" Breck asked, thick judgment deepening his voice. "You don't have a million dollars."

The man underestimated her, would he ever learn?

Smile. That's all she had to do. One of her big megawatt wonders always disarmed him.

"Sure I do," she said, ensuring to tip her head all the way back, under the guise of meeting his eye. The real reason? The column of her throat did it for him every time. There was something to be said for long-term, never-sated lust. "Forget you gave me a credit card?" Cue the eyelid twitch. Oh, she could gobble him up. Even with his mother on the other side of the nearby curtain. "Meet me New Year's Eve. Noon."

Bringing in one last New Year with him was a gift to herself. Selfish? Maybe, but he could always say no. He wouldn't say no.

"We said we weren't doing this anymore."

Yeah, how many times? She'd lost count.

Good thing... "We're not. This isn't that." She laid a bold hand flat on his hard chest and sighed. "Oh, it feels so wrong to walk away without taking you to bed."

"Coy..."

When he reached for her hand, she snatched it back. "Ah! We're not doing that anymore." Full smile illumination was the best defense against his grump. "Look at the smile, Stat. You're a sucker for the smile." Somehow it stretched higher. "How pretty is she..." She kissed her fingertips and rested them on his lips. "Saturday. Noon." She spun on the spot to sashay away, glancing back as she retreated. "You won't be disappointed, Stat."

"Never am, Coy."

He didn't shout. He didn't have to. Breck was a man among boys. A man proud of his place and certain of his future. Breck was sharp, to the point, and never had time to waste. Unless he was wasting it with her...

TWO

SHE SHOULD PROBABLY be nervous. Anyone else would be nervous. She wasn't. Anxiety didn't feature where Breck was concerned. Some might say they should've learned their lesson. "Some" being Breck; Breck would say it. No one else would dare comment on the conundrum that was their relationship... ex-relationship. Not in earshot of her and Breck anyway.

The large hotel room included a huge bed, seating area, and an ensuite family bathroom. Everything they needed. More than they needed actually. In the countless times they'd visited that room, she'd never once sat on the couch or armchairs. What was the need when the alternative was Breck's face? Man ate pussy better than any she'd ever known. That pride of his extended in all the right directions.

Might be more polite to situate herself on one of those chairs that Saturday, but she wouldn't. Again, what was the need?

She tied the belt of her silk robe in a loose knot. He'd given her the robe. And the lingerie adorning her body beneath. Breck was great at presents, generous, thoughtful, always sure—even when he couldn't be.

She swallowed some virgin wine, put the glass on the nightstand and perched herself on the bottom corner of the bed. Noon was right about...

The beep of the door lock signaled the time. Man, he was good. Always prompt. For her. Not always for other people. When it came to best boyfriend etiquette, he got top marks. Never made a promise he couldn't keep. Never stood her up. Never raised his voice. Never... Their list of nevers...

Wrong mood; switch it up.

As the door opened, her smile bloomed. She never had to force it with him, just being near to him filled her with a joy she'd never found anywhere else. A joy she couldn't conceal.

After one look at her, he took off his jacket to toss it over the back of the nearest armchair.

"We're not doing this anymore."

Was he telling her that or mocking their past conversations?

"I told you, this isn't that," she reiterated. "Really, Breck, you have to get better at listening."

As he crossed the room, loosening his cuffs, she climbed onto her knees on the edge of the bed, reaching for him as soon as she was able.

His cufflinks landed by her wine.

"This isn't that?" He released the belt of her robe to let it fall open, revealing the satin and lace beneath. The strength of his hands on her bare waist heightened her pride in her figure. Yeah, he loved it, and she worked hard to please him. "Looks like that."

"What something looks like and what it actually is are often two different things." Already she worked on the buttons of his shirt. "Use a little imagination, dearest."

Opening his shirt by sliding both hands across the width of his chest, she bit her lip to contain a whimper. How many times had she seen him naked? Too many to count. Yet every time contact gave her butterflies.

Skimming her hands up to link her fingers at the back of his neck, she coaxed him down to meet her lips in a quick kiss.

"You didn't have to pay a million dollars for this." When he swept her hair over her shoulders, admiring her as she tipped her head back, she knew she had him. To be honest, she didn't know how not to have him. With them, it had always been this. Automatic. Instinctual. Intuitive. "You could've just called."

"I could've walked into your office and stripped naked." She accepted his nod but boosted up for another short kiss. "I could've strode into your bedroom at B House and forced myself on you as you slept."

"Force? Never said no, never will. Why the theater?"

"It's not theater, it's a quid pro quo transaction."

"I'm not a gigolo."

"You don't care about the money and it's not going to you anyway, it's going to a good cause. And I didn't pay a million dollars for this: you did. Mmm…" Breathing against him, her knees left the bed, one, then the other as her legs wrapped around him. "Kiss me, Stat. You know what happens when you kiss me."

Losing his hand in her hair, he tightened it to a fist, tilting her head to counter his mouth locking onto hers. There it was. Him. Mmm. And when he moved, probably losing his shoes and socks, she did the work of opening his belt.

What was the harm of enjoying herself? No harm.

He lowered her onto her back, giving her the

perfect weight of him above, sheltering her in a position that never got old. The thick mass of him beneath her stimulating palm was certain in its insistence; she relied on that insistence and never had to work for it.

"You…" he said, separating their lips only to kiss her again. The fog of their need crowded the humidity that aided the instinct of their undulating bodies. "Never need a pretense."

"I know." The thick locks of his hair warmed her fingers. She pulled him in for another kiss, another. "I need you, Stat."

The frenzied kissing sped their hearts and their passions.

"So much for not doing this anymore," he panted with her, squeezing her breast.

"This isn't that."

"Then what is it?"

Thank God he'd asked. "I'm ovulating."

The motion of their kiss halted. He didn't pull away, didn't take his mouth back, he just breathed. Good, yes, Stat, process. He needed a minute, as expected. She'd wait.

Silence couldn't last forever.

Eventually he met her eye, taking nothing but his mouth from her. "You're ovulating."

She nodded. "According to my app. Isn't technology convenient?"

"And we're doing this because you want…"

"To have a baby." He'd know better than to expect anything less than direct from her. Raising her head, she kissed him again. "I need you."

He resisted her next shot at a kiss. "You don't need me, you need my…" On an exhale, his quick mind brought him up to speed. "You want to have a baby."

"It's my decision. Yes. I want to have a child. Your child, ideally. This isn't about money, I don't need a cent of the Breckenridge fortune. It's just… time for me."

"How long have you been thinking about this?"

"A while."

"Uh huh. We work in the same building." Talking it out wasn't exactly part of the plan. Not the perfect plan anyway. Still, knowing him, she'd anticipated this. "I have never ignored your calls."

"I didn't want to talk about it. I made this decision on my own; I want to be a mother."

"You going to marry me?"

"No," she said, wriggling her hand free to press a straight forefinger to his lips. "This is why I don't want to talk about it." Lifting her head to kiss him again, she left her finger there. "You like this part…" Another kiss. On the next, she slid her finger away to open her lips, letting her tongue just touch his before retreating. "We're good at this part. This part feels so good."

Pressing her feet to the mattress, she elevated her hips and his immediately pushed back, pinning her beneath him.

"Sequoia," he groaned, his head dropping.

She moistened her lips by his ear. "Would you rather I carry another man's child?" That got his attention. The ferocity in his eyes when they leaped to hers tumbled carnal energy in her belly. "If it's not your baby, it will have to be someone else's."

It hadn't occurred to her that any other man would be up to the job, or that Breck would want them to be.

Proving that point, he kissed her hard and hooked her knee into the crook of his elbow, slamming himself into her.

Her body arched, braced in a position that forced her to adjust to his mass. The satisfied smile that curved her lips gave her enough time to breathe and find her anchor again.

"Breck," she whispered.

"You will never carry another man's child," he growled, pulling out only to drive in deep again. "Sequoia Drury, you swear it to me right now."

"Mmm…" The whimper of her need became a whine. "I swear it."

He snatched her chin. "Swear what?"

Oh, this delectable man never failed to fulfill her every need.

"I swear I will never carry another man's child."

"Anything you need, you come to me."

She managed another smile, her body writhing, stimulating itself on the cock he'd bedded deep within her.

"Why do you think I'm here, Stat?"

"I never say no."

He said no all the time. Just… not to her. Again, exactly her point. She didn't have to think of any other route. Whenever she wanted something for herself or had something to give, Breck was the only man she'd engage. Hmm, maybe that wasn't the smartest word choice.

The slow rock of his pelvis grew in motion, from shorter pulses to longer thrusts, he did more than warm her up.

It had been a while for them. Though with them, it could feel like an age even if they'd only been parted a minute. Being with him, in their intimacy, she relished his deft fingers moving on her skin. How he was so entitled to touch her everywhere, to learn every crevice he'd already visited a thousand times.

"Breck," she murmured, moving with him and away in the rhythm they'd cracked a long time ago.

Shouldn't it be old by now? The sweet stimulation of his fingertips on her clit should be expected, yet her whole being reacted like it was the first time every time.

"Open your eyes, Coy."

Every time, every single time, when she did as told and looked into the man above her, the pleasure collided with overwhelming emotion that sucked her so deep, she couldn't breathe.

Yes. The word in her head came from her lips so many times the two got muddled. Want clenched in gratification and in the pound of orgasm, she called out to him.

Grabbing for his ribs, she dug her nails in deep and he growled, driving himself into her until he delivered his prize right where she wanted it.

THREE

BEFORE HIS BACK hit the bed, she crawled up it to lie down with her legs extended on the headboard.

"What are you doing?" he asked, perplexed.

"Gravity… it works."

"You're serious about this." His voice was closer, the direction—shifting her head just as his hit the pillow, he was soon on his side examining her. "You want this."

"I know myself."

"I know you do."

"I don't want to discuss it."

"We don't have to discuss it. I want you to have whatever you want."

"Because I want a child, you'll give me a child."

And for him, it was as simple as that.

"Yes. That doesn't mean I have no opinion or don't expect a say."

No, and being a man others listened to, he was used to his opinion being king.

"You're a good man. Smart. Conscientious. You are skilled and thorough and I adore you."

"Mm."

Suspicious too, though maybe with good reason.

"I don't need a partner."

"Don't I know it."

"You don't trust that I could raise a child alone?"

"You don't have to raise a child alone. Whatever you and they need—"

"I don't want money. Keep your money."

"I'm more than that," he said. "My family—"

"Never need to know it's your baby. It will stay between us. We'll be the only two people to know."

"This isn't something you decide alone. You don't need to—"

"I want to. You're adamant about your independence—"

"I'm adamant? Coy—"

"So we have one thing in common." Folding her arm, she brushed the back of her hand up and down his abdomen. "I can do this, Breck. I know I can."

"There's nothing you can't do. But why can't we do it together?"

Restraining her groan to a sigh, her fingers paused a moment, then she rolled away, off the bed to retreat to the bathroom.

"Do you want to shower?"

She didn't. Nope, her prize wouldn't be washed away yet.

"We done?" he called back.

"God, no. We're only just getting started."

She washed her hands and ran them through her hair. They continued down over her breasts to rest low on her belly. A child. He barely hesitated. She'd gone into this intending to be honest. Completely honest. That wasn't a conscious distinction, not really. She didn't lie to Breck. Never any need. He'd never once refused or rejected her. Look at the way he'd reacted with her honesty about ovulating. All in stride, that was Breck.

"Why me?"

"Why you?" she asked, frowning at her reflection.

"If not for the money, why pick me?"

That was almost offensive, yet a laugh warmed her throat. "You know why!"

Idiot didn't need it spelled out. That wasn't right, Breck may be many things, but he was no idiot.

"I'm sullen."

"And cranky," she called from the bathroom in agreement.

"I'm pedantic."

"And pernickety."

A pause.

"The depth of love I feel for you exists nowhere else in the world, Coy."

Going to hug the doorframe, her temple on the wood, she admired the man in their sheets. "And...?"

He sighed. "There's nothing I'd deny you."

Had to be in it to win it. Going back to the bed, she crawled up over him, coming to a stop straddling his hips.

"I want to have your baby, Breck." She touched his lips, trailing her fingers down his chin to his throat and onto his chest. "It's selfish of me."

"It's smart of you." He squeezed her hips. "You know I'm not going anywhere. We work together, share values—"

"No thanks to my family." When she tried to get up, he gripped tighter, holding her in place. "Breck..."

"You can have family. You do have family. You're a Breckenridge. It's only right you give birth to the first heir."

"My child doesn't want your company."

"My child will have every right to choose his or

her own path. Being the first of their generation doesn't tie them to anything. Nothing, Sequoia. Anything they want, they'll have."

"And you wonder why I say we don't need your money," she teased, rocking her hips. "If you had access, you'd spoil him." Her head went back on a rumbling laugh. "I dread to think how you'd indulge a girl."

"Not many of those in my family."

"She'd be the first Breckenridge princess."

"Is that a role you'd deny her?"

Her smile faded. "Don't do that."

"Do what?"

"That thing you do when you switch everything around." This time, she fought his grip and pulled his hands away to get onto her feet. "I'm educated. I'm responsible."

He rose to his elbows. "I didn't say you weren't."

"I don't have a wild lifestyle or dangerous addictions."

"Other than those Belgian peppermint chocolates." While her unimpressed eyes narrowed, he laughed. "Hate to think what would happen to the baby if they fought mommy for those."

"Breck," she groaned. "Don't be cute, we're fighting."

On an exhale, he sat up, swung his legs off the edge of the bed and lunged out to grab her hand, guiding her between his open thighs. "We're not fighting, Coy. No matter how we choose to raise this child, together or apart, with family support or without, we never have to fight about their existence. Our child will be loved."

Hmm, manipulation. "You're being kind to me, trying to wheedle your way in."

"Was I ever out?" he asked, his smile growing to a dazzle that caught her in the ribs. She wasn't the only one with moves. "I love you, Sequoia."

She snatched her hand back. "Don't say that to me." A whining groan itched her throat. "We're not doing that anymore."

"This isn't that."

And all she could do was breathe out. "Rankin Breckenridge…" Planting a hand on his shoulder, she pushed him down on the bed to climb on top again. "Less of the talking, more of the impregnating."

"Yes, ma'am."

FOUR

FIVE WEEKS LATER…

HER LONG DAY only got longer by the second. As Deputy Operations Officer working at Breckenridge HQ, her work was never done. Yeah, okay, so there were four Deputy Operations Officers, it wasn't all on her. But, huh, how come she was the only one at her desk still working long after office hours? In the low lighting of a floor that bustled all day, she liked the intimate quiet of her warm lamp in the evening, illuminating the papers beneath her pen.

"Is it true Breck's barred from your office and all meetings you attend?"

Looking up to the male voice, she smiled at Darroch Breckenridge, one of Breck's younger brothers.

"Not only that," she said, "he's required to maintain a minimum twenty-five-foot radius at all times."

He laughed, though it wasn't a joke, so she didn't get what was funny. "Why?"

"Reasons," she said and shrugged while stacking the papers to tap them on the desk, aligning them. "And we tend to have sex when he gets closer than that."

"Might be inappropriate in meetings."

"It might."

"Doesn't explain what's changed. You two have always been like that. The rest of us are so used to it, it's expected. Disappointing when you don't follow through."

Darroch could be serious when he had to be serious, and she could see through that amiable smile.

"Did Breck send you here?"

"No," he said, maybe a little too quickly. "Guys and I have a bet."

"Oh, what a surprise! The Breckenridge boys egging each other on, does today end in day?"

He laughed. "Ah, you know us so well. Coming to the Valentine's Ball?"

"Any excuse for a ball, right?"

"It's all for charity."

Yes, charity, another thing the Breckenridges were exceptionally good at. That was the trouble loving a man from such an incredible and altruistic family, there were so few things to stack in the con column.

"Didn't get your RSVP for my engagement party either."

"Did you ask Savanna yet?"

A sudden thwack spun Darroch around fast. The woman who'd just smacked his ass quickly tucked herself under his arm.

"Are you talking about me?"

"I'm always talking about you, Cherry," Darroch said and bowed to kiss her. "What are you doing here?"

"Am I not allowed to be here?" Savanna asked, feigning wide-eyed ignorance.

"You're always allowed to be here. In fact, I'd

recommend you spend all your weekdays here."

"Why's that?" Savanna threaded their fingers together. "Because you work here every day?"

"You'd be good for morale."

"Whose?"

"Mine."

"You two are adorable."

"We were just talking about the engagement party," Darroch said. "I asked you to marry me, didn't I? Did I ask you?" He picked up her hand to elevate her ring finger from the others. The size of that diamond left no doubt. "Yeah, I asked her... and I think she said yes... either that or she's fleecing me for the jewel."

"He asks me every day even though I'm always wearing his ring."

"It's a nice ring. Goes with every outfit. I'm just checking you don't forget."

"I wake up with him every morning, but he thinks I'll forget the man I love. The man who's promised me children."

He kissed her head and left his lips there in her hair. "Any time you want to get started..."

Of its own accord, Sequoia's head shook a little. "Alice Breckenridge should bottle it."

"Bottle what?" Savanna asked, pushing at her fiancé when his hands and lips started to get frisky. "Her parenting potion?"

"Whatever it is she feeds them to make them so..."

"Generous?" Darroch asked, snatching his woman back tight. "It's one of Savanna's favorite words."

"Except Brant." She pondered. "I don't know what happened there."

"Got to be an exception to every rule."

"I suppose that explains Tripp too."

Another Breckenridge brother.

"I'm meeting Alice tonight," Savanna said. "We're having drinks at Blaze, you should come."

"Oh no, I—"

"You're having drinks at Blaze? The restaurant attached to Crimson?" Darroch asked. "At Crimson Palace?"

The towering Rouge HQ building, also known as Crimson Palace, contained everything a person might need to have the night of their life. Restaurants, bars, hotel rooms, and, of course, the infamous Crimson nightclub. Its owner, Zairn Lomond, was a consummate host, and had found a complementary hostess in his fiancée, Roxie... something. She couldn't remember Roxie's last name. Remember? Huh. Had she ever known it?

"Yes," Savanna said. "In our private dining room."

He didn't sell his disappointment well. "You didn't come here to see me?"

"No." Savanna kept her chin high. "I'm waiting for your mother to finish a call."

"I'm heartbroken."

"I told you I wouldn't stop seeing Alice." Savanna gave him another nudge. "Anyway, less of the victim-act, you're partying with your brothers tonight! Would you prefer I just sat at home pining for you?"

"Always." Bold ran in the family. "Besides, it's not a party. It's a Tripp thing. I'm too old and responsible to party now. I'm going to be a husband soon."

"Oh, really. Too old to party? Your little get-together is at Crimson; one of the world's most infamous and debauched nightclubs." Even while the couple sparred, their love bloomed in their smiles. God, it was still so wonderful and new, they had a lot to look forward to. "In a building full of hot, semi-inebriated women, with your playboy brother working his magic all over the place."

"Exactly!" Darroch kissed her quick. "My playboy brother will handle the hot women."

"All of them?"

"If need be. Not like he's never done it before. Never wondered where he is when he disappears for days or weeks at a time? He has quotas to hit. Besides our party is upstairs, not in the club."

"Party?" Savanna crooked a triumphant brow. "In Tripp's private suite? That makes me feel much better. There are never hot, semi-inebriated women there."

That was pure sarcasm. Tripp's immediate periphery was always populated by gorgeous women.

Unconcerned, Darroch just laughed. "I've got the hottest woman alive right here. I'm done looking." His expression flattened. "We're having sex tonight, right?"

"We have a rule, remember?"

"Okay, call me and we'll go home together."

"Who's to say I'll be done with my girls before you're done with your guys?"

"Let me guess, Ms. Roxie Kyst will be there," Darroch said, squeezing Savanna. "So I might not see you for a week or two."

Kyst! Roxie Kyst, Crimson hostess, Rouge's ambassadress, the empress of all things connected to Zairn Lomond, CEO of the umbrella Rouge conglomerate.

"It's a possibility."

Sequoia interrupted the couple's flow. "It's a wonder I've managed to miss this woman everyone talks so highly of."

"Roxie?" Savanna asked. "You've never met Roxie? Oh, you have to meet her! Another reason to come with us tonight! You have to. I haven't spent enough time with you." They'd been introduced, that was about as far as it went. "Alice will be with us, it won't be too crazy, I promise."

Her eyes met Darroch's.

"You're one of us, Seq, you're family."

Which was his way of telling her Breck would be okay with it. Of course he would be okay with it. He didn't know how to not be okay with any of her choices... barring one.

"Not like I used to be."

"Breck's not an asshole. If you're mad at him—"

"Okay." She closed her laptop and stood up, ending that track of conversation. "I'd love to join you."

Would she? Maybe. Maybe not. One thing she didn't want to do was get into the nitty-gritty of her and Breck's non-existent relationship with one of his numerous brothers.

Everyone else had gone home. The building wouldn't fall down without her. Why shouldn't she have a little fun?

FIVE

"SEQUOIA DRURY, meet Roxanna Kyst. She prefers just Roxie."

The private dining space in Blaze was decked out just for them. Cocktails, canapes, a variety of goodies. All laid on by the striking beauty smiling at her, offering a hand of welcome.

"Breck's squeeze," Roxie said. "I've heard a lot about you."

"It's probably mostly true," she said, sitting as the others did too. Huh, alcohol, she hadn't drunk any since the previous year. She should've thought this socializing thing through to the end. "Tripp your source?"

"It's not like Breck would be," Savanna said, presenting her a cocktail.

She hesitated. "Anything virgin? I've been a little piqued the last couple of days."

"Sure," Roxie said. "You can have anything you want here, ma'am, anything at all. Baker!"

A guy scurried in. "Roxie?"

"We need virgin cocktails, sweetie, please." The

hostess looked at her. "Anything specific?"

"Something fruity?"

"Fruity we can do," Roxie said. "Anyone else? We want different food? We should have something more substantial. We're busy working women, we don't need to suffer this dainty crap."

"Roxie," Alice said on a laugh.

"What? And Jane's in LA for a few days…"

"So you won't be reminded you have a certain dress to fit into soon?"

"Exactly! You get me, Alice." Roxie's head dropped back. "We need something, I don't know… solid, not sensible."

A suggestion slipped out of her. "Pizza?"

"Ah ha!" Roxie snapped her fingers and pointed. "Pizza! Sequoia, good! Yes, but real pizza… Where will we get deep dish in this town?"

The Crimson helper still stood, expectant, waiting for instruction. "I can ask around."

Roxie raised a finger to Baker. "Oh, you know who's from Chicago? Miguel."

"The… staff chef?"

"Yes! Ask him… Want me to ask him?"

"No, I can ask him. I'm sure the kitchen could make—"

"Okay, but if they do, don't tell me." Roxie leaned back and patted her belly. "There's a figure under here our Emperor likes playing with. If I find out there's a limitless supply of Chicago pizza in the building… Phew, forget the wedding, he'll have to roll me out of bed."

"Okay," Baker said on a laugh that was joined by Roxie's smile. "Anything else?"

"Yes." Roxie grinned. "Keep being you, Baker. You're a superstar I wouldn't be able to live without."

"Yes, Roxie," he said like maybe he'd heard it

before and disappeared to do as told.

"I love that guy."

"You're kind to all of your staff," Alice said. "From what I hear, you're on first name terms with them all."

"Like you, you mean?" Another smile. "Z knows them all by name, I was backed into a corner. Can't be outdone, can I? Though with you in the building, Alice, the rest of us are put to shame."

"You're a very generous employer."

"Says the kindest woman in the whole world," Roxie said to Alice. "Z's got me beat there too. They walk all over him. He's not good at cracking the whip."

"Zairn listens," Sequoia said. "It's one of his best qualities."

"Until it gets me into trouble." Roxie's eyes narrowed. "I love meeting people who've known him a long time."

Startled, she didn't expect to be the instant focus of everyone. "Oh, I haven't known him... he's closer to my sister. Breck's known him forever. He has a lot of respect for Zairn, a lot of time for him."

"And Breck doesn't have a lot of time for a lot of people," Savanna said. "I think the only time I ever exchanged words with him was when Darroch was in the hospital."

Roxie reached for Savanna's hand on instinct. To comfort her?

"Darroch's okay now, isn't he?"

"Oh, yeah, that's all done and forgotten and... I'd like to know Breck better."

"My eldest has always been the most discerning," Alice said, taking some of the heat, thank God. "He's protective of the people he cares about and sees it as his responsibility to corral his brothers. He's also a teller of truth, often guiding others from unwise paths."

Except her... hmm, or maybe that should be himself.

"How long have you been together?" Roxie asked.

Wasn't the first time she'd been asked that question when—"We're not together. Haven't been for a while now."

"It can't be easy to be with a guy who doesn't say much," Savanna said, enjoying her cocktail. "Darroch never shuts up." The woman looked to Alice. "Not that I don't love that about him."

Alice laughed. "Darroch lights up with you, Sweet Savanna. You inspire that energy in him."

"Probably inspires energy in him when they're alone too."

Although Roxie feigned murmuring under her breath, the whole room heard.

"Roxie!"

Though Savanna chastised, Roxie's eyes widened in innocence. "What? So we're not allowed to talk about sex at all?"

"Not with his mother in the room!"

"I know what my boys get up to."

In general or specifics? Alice would accept her boys no matter what. If they needed to talk about anything intimate, their mother wouldn't shut them down. Still, the Breckenridge boys didn't burden their mother with details of their sex lives. Not Breck anyway. Another reason to be grateful he was a man of few words.

"How did you and Breck get together?"

"We're not together," she said again, noting the smile Alice concealed behind her glass. "What has he been telling people?"

"Oh, sweetheart, you know our dear Brecken, he says nothing."

"To anyone," Savanna said, swallowing a generous gulp. "Ever. Truth is, I'm scared of the guy. Everyone I've ever met is scared of him—everyone non-Breckenridge."

"I'm pretty sure there are some Breckenridges afraid too. Brant for sure."

Sequoia laughed. "People say that all the time." Alice got her focus. "I never understand how anyone can be intimidated by him."

"Because he's transfixed whenever you're near," Alice explained. "He's always been drawn to you. You're drawn to each other."

Something she couldn't deny.

"So spill it," Roxie said, stabbing an olive with a toothpick. "How'd you seduce him?"

"I didn't seduce him."

Did she? Maybe she did. Depended on the day of the week. When he was around, she was consistently in a state of seduced and, boy, was it mutual.

Roxie wasn't deterred. "You work for Breckenridge? Was he the big, bad boss and you the sexy, sultry assistant?"

"I never worked under Breck, not directly." What the hell! Why be cagey? "I worked with Ben." Breckenridge patriarch. Another glance at Alice awarded her comfort. "Mr. Breckenridge, Senior." The boys' father. Alice's husband. "I interned with him in college and took a paid position when I graduated." Given her baggage, God knew why he'd taken a chance on her. "He taught me everything I know. Everything useful I know."

And the rest she tried to forget.

"Ah…" Roxie's nod was slow in its understanding. "When you realized the original model wasn't available, you went for the next best thing."

"From the first moment he saw you, my boy was different," Alice explained. "I hadn't been there when you were introduced, but I knew something had changed. For the first time, he was distracted, I'd never seen him absentminded in my life. To this day, I can tell when you've had an interaction. You leave an imprint on him, my dear."

She should send him an apology card, maybe some flowers.

"So, hey, if you're so hooked on each other, how come you're not together?"

The trouble with Breck being so stoic was the world expected its answers from her. Sometimes that was fine; other times she couldn't remember the answers. Did she know the answers? Not always.

"Because life isn't as simple as that."

"My Casanova would argue with you there."

Baker came in with servers and fresh drinks. "Pizza's on its way."

"Excellent," Roxie said. "Thank you, all!" The servers disappeared. She was so grateful to have something to wet her throat. "Being together is always an option." Were they still on this? Roxie seemed to think so. "You just have to decide what you're willing to sacrifice."

"Unfortunately, it's not my choice."

"Breck won't sacrifice? What would he have to sacrifice?" Savanna mused. "The only thing I can imagine he wouldn't give up is his family and I won't believe for a second that Alice or any of the Breckenridges—"

"Of course not, they're an incredible family. It was my honor to be a part of their ranks for..."

Alice reached over to hold her hand. "You will always be a Breckenridge."

"You do like to adopt orphans."

Still holding her hand, Alice stroked her hair with the other. "You will always be my first daughter, Sequoia."

"Sure whoever Breck ends up with won't appreciate that," Roxie said.

"That will never be a concern," Alice said at peace with the situation. "I fully expect my eldest will never marry or have children."

"Don't say that, Alice," she said on an almost groan. "I wish only happiness for him. I want him to have everything he wants in life."

"And he's set his mind to what he wants, whether he can have it or not. You can set a man free, but you can't make him bolt. Together or not, his love for you endures."

"And I won't force him to endure what being with me would entail. I'd be unhappy. We'd both be unhappy."

"I know, sweetheart."

"*I* don't know," Roxie said. "Whatever's keeping you apart—"

"This isn't the best party conversation." Having only just met the woman, Sequoia wouldn't dump her whole sad history onto her. Savanna too. These were women in the prime of their lives and at the height of their love. "Tell me about you and Zairn."

"Our whole history's available on video in stereo sound," Roxie said, crossing her legs and propping an elbow on her knee, mouth wide to take in a deep breath. "But that won't stop me telling it. Have you ever heard of *Talk at Sunset*?"

"The TV show?"

"It all started there on a dark August night. Settle in, ladies, this might take a while..."

SIX

IF ALICE AND SAVANNA had heard Roxie's tale of love already, they were polite enough not to let on.

Pizza came, and, man, did it hit the spot. Deep dish, there was no better pizza. How long had it been…? A taste of home; one of the few that comforted her.

On a subtle stretch, she stood up. "Thank you, ladies. I've had an amazing time."

Getting to know Roxie and Savanna reminded her just how optimistic love could be. Savvy was good for Darroch. She'd never considered he needed to settle down in a hurry, not until his match came along.

"You can stay longer," Roxie said, leaping up. "We can go upstairs. You can spend the night. Plenty of room."

"I should be heading home too," Alice said, rising at her side. "I can drive you home, Sequoia."

"Thank you."

Alice Breckenridge was a woman like no other. If she wasn't as inherently gentle as she was, Sequoia might worry about getting the third degree on the homeward journey. Though Alice said "drive," the woman wouldn't be behind the wheel. Breckenridge money led to all kinds of luxuries that the family sometimes, unintentionally, took for granted. Language was different, words had other meanings, when that kind of legitimate means cushioned your life. Illegitimate wasn't the same. She should know.

Turning, intending to find her coat, a rush of heat flooded her head. And that was it, the last thing until opening her eyes to Alice and Savanna looming over her and she was... on the floor. Why was she on the floor?

Alice's hand was tight around hers. "Sweetheart, are you with us? Sequoia?"

"I..." When she tried to sit up, nausea put her down again. "Oh..."

Roxie crouched by Alice. "You passed out, honey. Are you hurt?"

"No, I—"

"She may have hit her head."

"Should I call an ambulance?"

"God, don't do that." Still woozy, she forced herself to sit up, closing her eyes for a little more stability. "I didn't eat anything today, I should've—"

"You ate here," Roxie said. "That pizza has strong-as-a-horse enzymes in it, this was no hypo."

"Don't try to get up." Savvy did her bit to keep her still. "Help's on the way."

And suddenly a head rush was the least of her concerns. "Help?" Uh oh. "What do you mean—" The door opened, bringing all women around and, of course, who was first through? "Breck—"

"What happened?" he asked, storming right on through the women, practically knocking them aside to crouch and cradle her head. "Are you hurt?"

"I'm not hurt. I'm fine."

"Coy—"

"Don't paw at me." Pushing his hands away did little to slow him down. "Breck—"

"You're on the floor."

"Only because no one will let me get up. I'm fine." And this was more than a little mortifying. "Honestly. I wouldn't lie to you."

"You're fine," he repeated to which she nodded, hoping that would be the end of it. How naive. "Both of you?"

A gasp. More than one. Not from her, no, from behind him, in the audience she couldn't actually see.

"Oh," Roxie said, "plot twist."

Did he really just...? Shit... Her jaw pushed to the side at the same time her eyes narrowed. And, no, he didn't leave any doubt as to what he meant. The stroking of her belly would clear up any uncertainty.

"There is no both of us."

This time when he tried to hold her down, she was more persistent in pushing his fawning away.

"You're not...?"

She couldn't say that. Not exactly. With his supporting arm around her, she got to her feet.

"Can we maybe not do this now?"

Blinded by his zeroed-focus, she had to twice shift her own gaze past him to remind the idiot they weren't alone. No, not an idiot, just not exactly with it. Had he been scared? She might mock him for that, internally, until considering how she'd feel on learning he'd just hit the deck for no reason.

"Coy—"

"Can I go home?"

"No," Breck said, surprising her with a bow that swept her off her feet.

"What the hell are you doing?"

"The doctor's on his way upstairs."

More than just the trio of women she'd spent the

evening with, there were now a large cohort of men in their party too. Breck bypassed all of them to carry her through the building.

The busy building.

No, they didn't go through the main restaurant, but they did cross from private corridors to the main central lobby. Plenty of people there. And with a lot of the walls to different units transparent, they probably made quite a spectacle for those in the various venues.

Maybe she should be angry. Indignant. Make a point of asserting her strength and independence. Except his actions weren't meant to diminish or question her capability, this was classic Breck. The man had to fix things. Had to act to remedy any wrong. Given the guy wasn't a doctor, he wasn't the best placed to remedy anything that might be broken. No. So what did he do? Overstretched in his reaction, heightened by fear, and coddled her.

Oh, how was he always so delicious?

She tipped her chin higher to murmur. "You don't have to carry me."

"You're not well."

"I'm fine," she said, though he was completely adorable. "I've passed out before."

"You have never passed out before."

And his certainty was... huh... "I haven't?" As he called the elevator, she searched her memory. "No, I don't think I have. Or, maybe, I just don't remember."

"All the more reason you shouldn't be living alone."

Her body arched as flirtation threatened her lips but... no, she wasn't supposed to be flirting with him or thinking about anything remotely... flirty around him.

"You're supposed to stay twenty-five feet away from me."

It wasn't until they were in the elevator that his

hooded eyes met hers. "This is serious."

"It is not serious. I fell over."

And had no memory of it, that was normal… wasn't it?

"Were you drinking alcohol?"

"I was not drinking alcohol," she said like she might to the school principal in high school.

Well, other people, she'd never been called to the principal's office. No principal would dare.

"Healthy, non-intoxicated women do not fall over for no reason." Okay, maybe. "And you claim there's no baby."

"I can't believe you asked me that in front of your mother. What were you thinking?"

"It's been a month and any time I try to get close—"

"We had this discussion. The baby is not your responsibility."

"You lied? There is a baby?"

"No! I did not lie," she said. This wasn't so cute anymore. "Would you stop scowling at me like that? Since when is judgment welcome in our relationship?"

"It's not judgment, it's…"

The elevator opened and out he went without finishing the thought. The long, carpeted hallway was one she recognized. High up in Crimson, they were on a private floor of suites, reserved only for Roxie and Zairn's special guests.

She didn't complain when he took her into one of the suites, or when he carried on through to lay her down in one of the bedrooms.

No, it was when he went for her shoes that she rebelled and pulled her legs away. "Don't take off my shoes."

"Why not?"

"We're not having sex."

Another voice interrupted. "Least wait until the doc's checked her out, bro. Have some class." Breck stepped aside and there was Tripp sauntering on in to join them. He came to sit with her, propping a fist by her hip to lean in and kiss her temple. "You should've called me."

Their eyes met. "I'm not pregnant."

"That's not what I'm hearing."

"Because your brother opened his big, stupid mouth in front of people. There's no baby—" Except this was Tripp. "I don't think there's a baby—I don't know if there's a baby."

"You took a test?"

"No," she said. "This is one of those things that happens whether you know it or not. I figure at some point, or not, I'll know."

"You were scared to be disappointed. You want to be pregnant."

"Conning your brother into giving it a shot once was difficult enough. I don't have it in me to hoodwink him twice."

Yeah, okay... so she could, it wouldn't take much. It was distancing themselves afterward that was the real hard part.

"You do have it in you, Seq. If it's something you want, you'll get it." Tripp's smirk grew. "Not like my brother's ever fought you off."

From each other, their focus went to the stern man standing at the foot of the bed. Okay, he was cute again. All angry and grumpy, she missed the days when it was her job, and delight, to loosen him up.

A whole stream of people barreled through the suite disrupting her burgeoning fantasy. They heard them coming before the cascade of bodies burst in.

"Ben is on his way."

"This is insanity," she said, pushing herself

upright while Tripp adjusted the pillows so she could sit against them. "No one has to worry. No one has to—"

"You're carrying the next generation of Breckenridge in there." Darroch's arm went around Savanna to pull her against him. "Guess ours will be the spare."

All suspicion suddenly turned on the affianced couple. Good. Let's see how they liked it.

"We're not pregnant," Savvy said, elbowing her love. "And, Gentleman, you're not being kind."

"What's not kind about that? I can't wait to meet the little guy."

Caber, another brother, didn't let that one slide. "Might be a girl."

"A girl."

The sentimentality in Alice's voice cracked her heart.

"Alice, I really don't know. I don't."

"The gender?" Caber asked. "Or if it exists?"

Tripp, still close, back to the others, showed sympathy in his smile, but what could he do?

"Nothing you can do to get them all out of here, Priest?" she asked. "You've never hesitated to clear a room before when necessary."

"Think if I use my usual tactics, Breck might rip my head off."

Think? Might? No, darling Tripp, there'd be no question about it.

Giving in, this wasn't going away on its own. "I don't know if there's a baby. There might be a baby. I don't think there is, but…"

"You never took a test?"

The question was valid. No, in the regular course of their lives women didn't go around taking pregnancy tests for no reason. Except… Breck hadn't given an inch, his tense muscles remained tight, and it wasn't fun to see him so scrunchy.

"We have tests upstairs," Roxie said.

"We do?" Zairn asked.

Roxie rested her weight against him. "Come on! You think with all the sex that goes on around here, Jane isn't doing random spot checks? I think we get them wholesale."

"Jane's in California."

"What does that matter? She doesn't have to be in the state to hold us accountable," Roxie said. "She's attentive, she notices things."

"What kind of things?"

"None of your business, Skippy." Roxie fixed on her. "You want a test, Sequoia?"

"Yes," Breck answered.

Tripp kissed her again and stood up. "Let's give these two a minute."

"We'll wait in the living room," Savvy said, using two hands on Darroch's to tug him that way. "Should we send the doctor in?"

Normally, she wouldn't stand for any man dictating the moment, but Breck was so clenched, some alone time would do him a favor.

Alice touched his arm and he raised it a little, that was as much acknowledgement as his mother got.

When the door closed, she arched a brow. "You see what you did."

"What I did? Why haven't you taken a test?"

"I already answered that."

"You didn't."

Coming around the bed, he didn't ask permission to grab her ankles and toss off her shoes. Throwing them aside, he wasn't shy about driving his hands up her thighs to push her skirt as high as it would go. Before she could ask, he snatched her head in both hands and planted his mouth on hers.

Yeah, he was mad. Their kisses were a whole other language. The push of his tongue and the strength in his grip proved his fear too, his longing. A month apart, without any direct contact... how long had it been since they'd gone a month cold turkey? Had they ever?

SEVEN

SHE FOUGHT TO dip her head back enough to speak. "If we're having sex, lock that door or text Tripp. Your mother walking in is one thing, but if Ben's on his way—"

"We're not having sex." The tension ebbed just a little as he sat back, still holding her head. "You're going to tell me why you haven't taken a test."

The hold became more of a caress until he was stroking her hair back from her cheeks over and over.

"Because if it's negative, the hope goes away."

"Did I tell you it was a one-shot deal?" he asked. "Hell, if I said that, would you believe me?"

No, probably not, the last few minutes were a good indicator of their typical restraint around each other, or more accurately, their lack thereof.

"Why do we have to know so urgently?" Somewhere in the course of the night's dramatic events, they'd become "*we*" again. How did that happen? That mindset needed to be turned on its head, quick, for both of their sakes. "Why does it matter?"

"Because there are steps you should be taking if you're pregnant. If we know, we can make adjustments to—"

"I take vitamins. I eat right. Exercise. You know these things about me."

"And alcohol?"

"I stopped drinking at Thanksgiving."

When her drive to procreate ramped up. Hoping the possibility was on the horizon, she'd taken steps to give them their best shot.

"Work?" he asked. "You've been in late every night for weeks."

A busy mind meant less speculating. "There are things to do and I love my job. Gil's leaving at the end of the month."

"Yes."

Since the opportunity presented itself... "And I don't know that we need a new person, you should promote from within."

"If you have a suggestion..." He was edging nearer to scrunchy until he figured her out. "If you want the job, it's yours. Can you shoulder two divisions?"

"Just to be nice, I won't slap you in the face for your doubt. I think choosing someone internal makes more sense than breaking in a stranger. I'm assertive, I'm loyal, I'm tenacious—"

"You're my girl. I was sold before you started talking." His fingers were slower in combing through her hair. "Love, you could have my job if you wanted it. Hell, if you wanted Dad's job, I'd find a way to give it to you." His other hand rested on her thigh, high up, so his fingers could graze her abdomen. "How will you handle two divisions with a baby?"

"Women work and have children all the time. How can you doubt me?"

"I do not doubt you. But this is a good time to

remind you there's no need to do it alone."

"Breckenridge have daycare."

"They do. And would you expect me to walk past my child every day and fail to acknowledge them?"

Perhaps he'd meant that to be somber or sharp, instead a laugh whispered past her lips. "I think it would be easier for you than it would be for your mom."

And as he explored her, his probing curled around her heart. No matter the laughter, he could read deep truths within her that even she couldn't interpret.

"You're worried about your father."

All frivolity fled.

"Why did you do that?" she asked, mood flipped on its head. "We were having a perfectly nice conversation." She tried to get up. "Please don't talk about him."

He caught her hips to clamp her down. "We can protect you."

"That's not your job."

That truth didn't make a jot of difference to him. "How far do you think he'll go?"

"With my father, I'd never venture a guess. He'll always surprise us."

"My brothers own one of the largest security firms in the country—"

"I know that."

"We can have you surrounded twenty-four, seven."

"That's not the way I want to raise my child."

"What's more important than their safety?" The sheer struggle written in his expression cut her deep. He literally couldn't figure it out. No matter how hard or long he thought about it, he'd never come up with an answer because there wasn't one, not a happy one. "Coy, I'll keep you safe."

"I am not your burden to bear." How many times

had she said it? "This isn't your responsibility. If he doesn't know it's your child—"

"I don't give a fuck who the father is," he said. "Look me in the eye, Coy, and tell me it would matter. Tell me I'd fight any less for you, and this baby, whether it was biologically mine or not."

He'd move heaven and earth for her. All those corny lines about a guy switching the sun and moon and rearranging the stars? Yeah, it was all talk, no man would be capable. None except her Breck.

Any other guy might say he didn't care about parentage. Any other woman would be right to hesitate. Except Breck's squadron of brothers weren't biologically related, some were, some weren't, and it didn't matter. Genes were irrelevant, love was love, family was family. They were all Breckenridges just the same.

"This wasn't supposed to happen this way." Everything was all screwed up. Why couldn't life just go to plan? "People weren't supposed to know. Why did you have to open your big mouth?"

"If you'd talked to me in person…"

"Oh, no, don't put this on me. It was private. It should've been private. I told you it was private. We're private."

"My family don't lie to each other. Did you think they wouldn't notice you pregnant or with a baby? How long would it take them to ask?"

"Haven was right, I should've used a sperm bank. It worked for her."

"Then what? Your father is persistent." He linked their hands. "Any child you have will be at risk."

"He's not at risk." In offense, she snatched her hands back. "My child will grow up healthy and happy. We don't know that my father will be interested at all. You know how he feels about promiscuity."

"You're not promiscuous."

"You know what I mean."

"How he feels about sex before marriage when it comes to his little girls? Yes, I do. Is that the—you think because this child will be born out of wedlock he'll let it slide?"

Archaic way of putting it, but accurate. "His rules are specific."

"And you've never played by them."

She had, actually, for years, as a child, before realizing there was another way.

"This is my life. I will live it how I want to live it."

"Except you won't because you won't marry me."

"That's my choice, not his."

"You make it because of him..." Pouncing up from the bed, he stalked to the glazed wall to gaze out over the city. "Coy, we've played this game for too long."

"Which is why we need a clean break."

"You think that's possible?" He spun around, throwing an arm out to his side. "I stare at you all goddamn day. I can't hear myself think when you're in the building."

Which was all the time. "Are you telling me to quit my job?"

"No," he said, stalking back to her. "You belong to Breckenridge and you always will. I'd never let anyone else hire you. If they tried it, we'd initiate a hostile takeover not long after."

The words "Breckenridge" and "hostile" were contradictory. Trust her Breck to be the first breaking the mold, and for her to be the one prompting it. Such a good family didn't deserve to be connected to someone like her.

Oh, it was fraught, and so much could go wrong, but she sighed. "That's a ridiculous statement. It's arrogant, misogynistic, abusive behavior…"

Again, he sat with her. "And you can't get enough of it. You know you belong to me, Coy. You want me to own you, like you own me." His fingers brushed across her cheek. "I'd never let any man take you from me, including your father."

Her stomach lightened. He always did that, got close and inspired need, hope… naïveté.

"This responsibility isn't on your shoulders," she stated. "I've told you that. How many times have I told you that? We've had this conversation. We are through, Breck, finished, over, finito. My business is no longer your business."

She hated being abrupt. Though it wasn't like he couldn't take it. In his job, he dealt with tough customers every day. The role demanded he bear responsibility for corporate Breckenridge. And at home? He shouldered responsibility for every one of his brothers. You know that saying about the camel and the straw? She wouldn't be the straw. That decision was clear cut when it came to them.

Ending their relationship was the most difficult thing she'd ever done. Until then anyway. It wasn't about her biological clock, not as such. Having children had always been an ambition. For years, it was one of those things out there on the agenda that they just hadn't got to yet. And when the time came? It could only be him. Why could it only be him?

A knock at the door interrupted his scrutiny. Opportunistic, because what could he say?

Roxie poked her head around the door. "The doctor's here. Alice is getting twitchy, you need to see this guy."

"Yeah, send him in."

"Coy—"

"We'll finish this later."

So much of her time was spent thinking about what he'd do for her. She spent little acknowledging just what she'd do for him. Although he couldn't see it, putting up barriers protected him. Regardless of what he thought of her, she would act in his best interest. And when it came to her father, she was a world authority.

"Do you want me to stay?" Breck asked.

"No." Her gaze switched to Roxie. "Would you stay with me?"

"Yes, absolutely. I'll stay."

Whatever his thoughts, he kept them to himself. In typical Breck fashion, he stood up straight, expression inscrutable, and stalked out like he had somewhere else to be. Big faker. Man had nowhere else to be. Nowhere was ever more important than right next to her.

"Are you sure you want me?" Roxie came closer to the bed. "We just met tonight, and—"

"Everyone else out there is a Breckenridge. I don't want to impose, but from everything I've heard you take supporting people seriously, especially women."

Roxie's cheeks plumped. "We're going to be fast friends." The woman went around the bed to climb on the unoccupied side. "Anything I should know?"

The doctor came in carrying a bulky first aid bag. "Ms. Drury, I understand you took a tumble."

Yes, many years ago she'd tumbled head over heels for a man she could never have. So much for her straightforward plan. This wasn't how it was supposed to be. The pregnancy was supposed to be quick and easy, the getting pregnant part anyway. She'd figured when it was done, when he'd done his duty, she'd have what she wanted and no one would get hurt. Now it was all complicated and messy. How was she going to clean this up?

EIGHT

SITTING THIGH TO THIGH with Roxie on the bathroom ottoman, the pair fixated on the unused pregnancy test balancing on their knees.

"You don't have to take it," Roxie said. "We can just tell them it was negative."

The solidarity was appreciated though not realistic.

"I work in the same building as various Breckenridges. If it came out positive, how long do you think I could keep that secret?"

Even if she managed to hide her bump, if she got one, hiding a child would be harder.

"God, I'm an idiot." Sweeping the test to Roxie's lap, she got up to march to the mirror and set her hands on either side of the sink. "What was I thinking choosing him?"

"From what I know of the eldest Breckenridge, which, granted, isn't much, it wouldn't matter who the father was. If you walked in there pregnant, he wouldn't ask questions. Why don't you want to know?"

"I told Breck I wanted a child the day we... you know."

"And he was okay with it? You planned this?"

"I planned to have a child. I thought it would be an easy in and out." So to speak, no pun intended. "I told him I was ovulating."

"Just like that, and he was okay with it? Have you discussed it before?"

"I took advantage of him, didn't I? I know he's in love with me. It's not possible for him to refuse me. I needed something and I went to him. It's in my bones, it's not my fault, it's instinct."

That was all excuses; it was her fault. Though, honestly, could she imagine any other man touching her? Ever? Maybe Alice wasn't far wrong about the prospect of Breck's romantic future. Hers might wind up the same.

"Looks like love to me. So what's the problem? The Breckenridges are amazing."

"Yes, they are. My family aren't so scrupulous. Breck and I finished our relationship because I didn't want my father to take advantage of such an amazing family. I don't want them tainted; I won't be responsible for that. They don't deserve it. My father's one entitled S-O-B. That's why I told Breck not to tell anyone about the baby. Now everyone knows, I can't envision how this will play out. Yes, there was always a chance my father would find out I had a child, but there was no need for him to ever know it was Breck's child."

Behind her, reflected in the mirror, Roxie approached. "Your dad isn't just a scrounging loser, is he?"

An ironic, despondent laugh escaped on her next breath. "My father is a respectable member of society..." or so the script went. "That's what he wants the world to think. He goes to great lengths to hide the truth."

"What's the truth?"

"That he's into about every shady scheme going; he's responsible for instigating most of them. On top of that, he's a bully and a tyrant. Not qualities anyone wants for their children's grandparent." What was she supposed to do? Just never have children? Maybe that would've been the smarter choice. "I broke ties with him years ago."

"You think he'll reappear in your life if he finds out you're pregnant?"

"I think he keeps tabs on me. I may have cut ties with him, I can't say he's done the same with me."

"Tell him to go to hell. Acre and Axon have—"

"I know." Another snicker flavored her breath. "I know. I know. The Breckenridge family have been my life for years. Look, it's all about appearances, it starts that way anyway. You don't know how my father operates, how he weasels his way in. If I get married, he'll be there."

"He doesn't have to be. Acre will keep him away. Z and I have contacts—"

"Don't you see it doesn't matter? Whether he gets an invite or not, he shows up. There's a scene, a ruckus, scandal."

"The press don't have to be there either. Zairn and I can help with that; it's our area of expertise. We get a lot of practice."

"The press? I don't care about the press. Yes, that would be embarrassing, and the news would get further faster, but the media doesn't matter. What my father does is illegal, and he's a master of manipulation. Tying my name to the Breckenridges is the same as tying his to them. The Breckenridges are wholesome, their name means something. It's goodness, kindness, it's the best of humanity."

"You think your father would ask Breck for a

favor?"

"More than one. Just standing next to each other would be enough to get the feds interested, and my father won't care if the Breckenridge name is tarnished. Association is enough. And my father could do with some legitimacy right now. My father is the lowest of the low, he'd waste no time and use the Breckenridge name to get what he wanted. He's not beyond blackmail or bribery. I'm in the muck, have been since I was born. I won't do that to my child; I won't do it to Breck."

"This is conjecture, you don't know for sure that your dad will—"

"I do. He's in my whole life. Control gets him off. He needs to be a part of every little thing. When I refused to join the family firm, he systematically attempted to destroy every part of my life. My professors were marking down papers, and I couldn't get an internship anywhere. I applied and applied, nothing. Until Breckenridge. Ben was so nice, the interview went great. It had been so long since anyone interacted with me without fear or anger."

"You can see where his boys get it from."

"He was so kind, so open. We were saying goodbye and stood up. I could've kept my mouth shut, maybe I should've. Who knows where I'd be now if I just walked out of there."

"You told him about your dad."

She nodded. "It didn't feel right concealing something so important, not in the face of Ben's kindness. He had to know if he took me on what they may face. Forewarned is forearmed, so I thought."

"What did he say?"

"He sat us down and poured me a drink that I really shouldn't have drunk in the middle of the day." Roxie's warm smile followed hers. "I told him everything." Looking back it felt long ago, years had passed since then. Yet she'd never forget Ben's patience, his generosity. "Took hours and he didn't rush me, never once looked at his desk or answered his phone. After I started, I couldn't stop. It all spilled out, I don't know why he listened."

"Because he's Benedict Breckenridge, and, you know, Alice would've kicked his ass if she found out he'd turned you away."

Damn straight. "I apologized for wasting his time, with the interview. No one else would even look at me, I appreciated him being patient. I should've been upfront the moment I walked in. I told him to expect a call from my father. That as soon as he got it..."

"Let me guess, Ben said he'd tell your dad to go to hell."

She rested her hip on the vanity and took a deep breath. "He said my father had already called three times that week. Ben knew who I was from the second I walked in and he saw me anyway, listened anyway."

Roxie's incredulity matched what she felt that day too. "Wow, and he never said a word?"

"No," she said, laughing at the memory. "He just let me go on and on."

"Did he hire you on the spot?"

"He took me home for dinner first."

"To Alice?"

Gosh, a million years ago. "To support not judgment."

"That's when you met Breck."

"Not that night, but not long after."

"Love at first sight?"

In a way, she couldn't deny that. Except... "When are things ever that simple?"

Lust at first sight for sure, though at Breckenridge House there was plenty to lust over.

"You broke up with Breck to protect him. As a

boyfriend, you're not permanently linked, that's why you broke up with him. To protect him. You don't believe he would do the same for you?"

"No one can protect me from my father."

"What comes next? One way or the other you have to do this test; the truth is the truth. The more time you have to get used to this, to prepare for this, the better."

She'd been putting it off for all the reasons mentioned, everyone was right. Including Roxie. Her newest friend held the test aloft for a moment before holding it out. Yes, they did have to know.

"Okay, okay, I'll do it."

The moment the plastic touched her fingers her heart beat a little faster. This was it. Pee on the stick. How hard was that? Not hard at all if she didn't think about the consequences of an affirmative answer. That was what she wanted, what she had wanted until Breck opened his mouth. Right. She'd pee on the stick and deal with whatever came after, one step at a time.

NINE

NO BABY.

She wasn't disappointed. It worked out for the best. They'd swerved a bullet. Her idea to have Breck's baby was crazy and she'd—where was he?

After the pregnancy test came out negative, she'd excused herself from Roxie's and gone home. Not much left to party for after her non-news killed the mood. The memory of that night wouldn't die. She'd have happily gone her whole life without walking into a room full of expectant Breckenridges only to disappoint them. Alice, especially, was ready to meet the next generation. The woman didn't say it, wouldn't, but an infant would've been the greatest gift.

Breck tried to join her when she'd declared her departure. The others expected him to go home with her because it was them. Them. That was exactly why she refused his company.

Fuck it.

Yes, okay, she was disappointed. Why did it feel so shameful to admit that even secretly in her own private thoughts? Maybe because all she'd have to do was pout at Breck, confess her dejection, and he'd do whatever it took to make it better. The solution was within reach, but she couldn't pursue it, couldn't take advantage of him... again.

They'd dodged a bullet, hadn't she literally just thought that? Guilt was too tame a word. What kind of horrible, despicable person—maybe she should quit her job. Uh huh, sure, how many times did that idea crop up? Every time her hormones salivated over the man working at the opposite end of the floor, that's how often. It wouldn't happen. She'd never follow through.

What a coward. It was one thing to be aware that her proximity caused him damage. It was another to relieve that damage by never being near him again.

She was a junkie. Breck Breckenridge was her drug. Rehab didn't exist for her addiction, and the most shameful part? Even if it did, she wouldn't go. Her preoccupation with him was her life. Seeing him, even for the briefest moment, was what she lived for. How sad was that?

Which brought her to the question of the day: where was he?

Not just that day either. A week had passed since their Crimson catastrophe and she hadn't seen him once since then. Not once. Jonesing for him had never been this bad... or maybe it had and she'd repressed the torment. How much longer could she live like this? Talk about cruelty.

For the last five days, she, as usual, worked in her office at Breckenridge HQ, pretending she wouldn't catch glimpses out to the executive floor any time he went in or out of his office. Or she would pretend, if he'd shown up to give her the chance. In a normal week, she'd see him regularly. Even if they didn't interact, the game went on. That week, she hadn't seen or heard a whisper of him. A *week*. Had she mentioned no sightings for a week?

One day of absence was an anomaly. Two was strange. Three was curious. Four was concerning, and they were all the way at day five now. Friday. Yep, that meant verging on panic.

She could ask. Any of the Breckenridges would answer. If it was her place to know where he was, which it wasn't, because they weren't together.

Ahh!

Or she could call him. He'd pick up. In a real pinch, she could go to Breckenridge House, no one would get in her way. She had rights. No, no she didn't. Well, she did, though she shouldn't. Why? Because they weren't together.

If Breck wasn't at work, he had to be home. Maybe. No. Logic didn't work. He was supposed to be there, in the building, that was the logical answer to where he'd be. Except he wasn't.

Goddamnit, the man's life wasn't her business. Something was wrong with her, way deep down in her screwed-up psyche. What the hell was a clean break? It wasn't staring across the floor at his office waiting for someone, anyone, to go in there. To give her some hint—

She closed her laptop in the same snap of finding her feet.

This was insane. If something happened with the family, some tragedy, none of them would be in. Everyone was in. Except him. Whatever was going on was Breck related, and damnit, Breck related was her related. He wouldn't hesitate to assume the same if the situation was reversed. Hell, no way he'd wait five days to quiz her.

Ben was in some meeting, and going to the top as a first stop was more than dramatic. Darroch would tease her. Not that she couldn't take it, but he wouldn't be the best person to break bad news.

It couldn't be bad news.

No.

Someone would've come to her with bad news… wouldn't they?

If it was medical, the whole family would be at Breck's bedside and she wouldn't have seen any of them. She should get friendlier with Savanna. Alice was available to her twenty-four, seven, but the wonderful woman didn't have time to get held up by gossip.

This wasn't gossip, this was something. Gossip didn't keep Breck from his office for a week. What could be happening in his life that didn't affect the other Breckenridges? Another woman? Ha, funny. That was firmly in the "no way" column. No, it had to be something…

Sheesh, talk about FOMO. Something was going on in Breck's life, he might need support, and she was out of the loop. She was his loop, who did he think he was cutting her out? Radio silence was not okay and she'd tell him that… if he ever graced her with his appearance again. Guy better wear a helmet and pads if he did because this was not okay. Disappearing on her was not okay. Worrying her, scaring her, he'd need a shield and a stick to survive when she caught up with him.

Ward was in, but she bypassed his office to march into another.

"Where is he?" she demanded of the man behind the desk. He pushed back in his seat. "Caber, I swear to—"

"Tripp wins the pool. How does he always do that? You women have to stop confiding in him, puts him at an unfair advantage."

She hadn't talked to Tripp since leaving Roxie's last Friday night.

"So you're playing a game? Breck's supposed to be the sensible one. He wouldn't take a whole week off work for a bet. Is the point to rile me?" Talk about conceited. "This isn't about me. This time off—

"Not time off," Caber said, shaking his head as he picked up his pen to tap it on the desk. "He quit."

If someone so much as sneezed in her direction, she'd go down. Bowled over didn't begin to cover it.

He couldn't mean... "Quit what?"

"Breckenridge."

After the words bedded in, her smile reacted. "Bullshit," she said on a burst of laughter. "Is that your bet? You think I would fall for that? Not a chance he'd—"

"He quit," Caber said with a slight nod. "All the way. He no longer works for any Breckenridge company and claims he never will."

Should she be startled or devastated? "Why?" the question just popped out. "Ben would never..." Maybe she should've gone straight to the top; this was insanity. "What could possibly have happened? Was there a fight?"

Arguments or disagreements might cause tantrums and forever rifts in her family, it would be alien for the Breckenridges. With them, respect and communication were everything.

"No. He's just through. Says he has priorities."

"He loves his job. His family. Working with—he loves his job." She knew the man just as well as his mother, better in some arenas, yet she had nothing. No explanation. Her mind was blank, completely empty. Why would he choose this? "Is he stepping back to give the rest of you the chance to...?"

To what? The Breckenridges made space for each other. Alice could deal with hurt feelings and Ben controlled the beast's ego. They were caring parents, involved, they didn't favor one son over another. If someone else wanted a crack at something, they'd give them the chance. Breck wouldn't stand in the way of his brothers' ambition either. It was a sight to see when they conversed; the family actually respected each other for real.

"It was completely his choice," Caber said. "Kinda came from nowhere, but, yeah, he's sure. This is what he wants."

No Breckenridge would stand in the way of another following their chosen path, even if that path steered them away from the family.

"Why?" There it was again. "What possible reason...?"

Maybe it was a medical emergency and no one had noticed his psychosis. Could be he'd hit his head or swallowed something toxic.

Caber shrugged. "He has a plan."

And now she was just incredulous. "What plan?"

His lips widened in a smile. "You expect me to answer that?"

No. Because on top of everything else, Breckenridges kept each other's confidence.

This was the Twilight Zone. "It's a secret plan?"

"I don't know if it's secret, just know I won't be the one opening my mouth."

Because he didn't want the force of her wrath? That meant it was a stupid plan. And who better to tell him that?

"No, you're right," she said. "I'll go to B House and browbeat him myself. Quit? Breckenridge? He is Breckenridge!"

"And while I'm over here doing my best not to be offended by that declaration..." Uh huh, not so much. Caber didn't know how to be offended. Right then it seemed all he could do to hold in his amusement.

"I'll tell you, he's not at home."

Another curveball. Although...

"He found another job already? Where?" Because she wouldn't hesitate to walk in there either, security clearance or not. In this state, she'd storm right through the damn walls. "You don't have to tell me, but I'll be sitting on your mother's front steps until he gets back from—"

"Might be waiting a while, he's not living at the house either."

New job, new home, what next? She dreaded to think. Could involve a woman without a weight of baggage dragging him down. Did she want him to be happy? Yes. Did she want to imagine him bonding with anyone but her? Definitely not.

Hell mend any new woman in his life who tried to take him from his work or his family. Both were so intrinsic to his identity, the true him would cease to be if this new love interest tried to separate him from either.

"Are you going to tell me where he is or do I have to turn the thumbscrews on one of your little brothers? Ward's in his office, within easy reach..." She'd be wherever Breck was in a snap. Providing it was in the city, the state—he wouldn't go to another country for a job... would he? He was good, amazingly good in many areas of life, another nation might offer him a better outlook. "Stonewall me and I'll file a missing person report."

His head tilted. "Your instinct's to go to the cops? Where'd you learn that?"

Not from her family anyway. "Ha-ha, stop trying to change the subject. I'll find him. One way or another—"

"He's at Darroch's," Caber said, dragging a cellphone across his desk. "I'll text you the address."

So Breck wasn't hiding from her? Good. He

should be smarter than that.

"Darroch's? Isn't Savvy's place a studio?"

She'd never been there, but had heard tell.

"A loft," Caber said, pushing his phone away to show more amusement. "But, yeah, no walls on their bedroom. Roch's been a little stretched this week."

It was almost funny that Darroch Breckenridge lived in such a small place. He could afford the best, palatial, yet he was happy where his woman was, happy to be with her. Just like Breck would—no, she wouldn't cut him any slack. Not until this secret plan was out in the open.

TEN

KNOCKING AT SAVANNA'S place only heated her blood. It was anger. Maybe it was anger. Frustration? Annoyance? Impatience? He better not feed her some line about secret passions or artistic ambition. He didn't conceal some hankering for a life on stage or blasting into space. They'd done talking through the night too many times to count and he'd never once mentioned being held back from fulfilling a childhood dream by any obligation to the family firm.

But it had to be something that drastic. Why else would he quit not only his career, but his family legacy?

This was so out of left field. It had to be medical. Had to be. Man better be in some kind of fugue state if he believed she'd let him throw away everything he'd worked to build for the Breckenridge future.

The loft door opened and there he was: the man she'd missed all week. That in itself was enough to shake her head. What was he doing answering the door?

"You should be too busy to answer the door," she said, fighting against gritting her teeth. "Have you contracted a brain eating parasite?"

"Coy—"

"Ah!" she exclaimed, prodding him hard. "No. We don't know each other. We're complete strangers. I don't know any man who would be so reckless and ridiculous. I must've misheard your brother because there's no way it's true, you quit the firm?"

"Coy—"

"You don't quit your job without talking to me—" She looked down. "Why am I still on this side of the threshold?"

He stepped aside and in she went, ascending into an open plan space with stairs to the far right up to, what she guessed, was the wall-less bedroom. What a set up.

"Would you like a drink?"

Like this was just any normal visit. Breck's unwavering calm had never unnerved her, not until right then. This was like talking to a stranger.

"This is where you're living? Why?" Spinning on the spot, she tried to see into the man she knew so well, who she thought she knew. Nothing. She got nothing. "Are you on drugs?" She went to take his hand. "You can tell me. I'll support you through anything. We all will."

Did she really believe he was strung out on some foreign substance? No. Though it could be a preferable motive versus whatever truly prompted this.

"Only thing I'm hooked on is you, Coy."

"I shouldn't have come here first. I should've gone to your mother to arrange an intervention." If it wasn't medical or chemical—"Are you being blackmailed? Did someone bribe you to make space or sabotage—"

"You know me better than that."

The Breckenridges had an all for one thing; what happened to one, happened to them all. Someone else would have a clue what was in his head, should have a clue, better have a clue. As it stood his intention was murky. Good thing she was back in the loop, sort of, no one was better equipped to get answers. If she struck out, answers didn't exist.

"Didn't you hear me? I don't know you at all, Strange Man from Outer Space," she said, whirling around to march to the couch and throw her purse down. To be honest, she didn't know where to begin. "You're living here? How do you expect that to work out? You're crashing your brother's life. Are you worried about him? Is it Savvy? You don't trust her?"

"No, no one's worried about Darroch or Savvy."

"Can't say the same about you, Stat. If you didn't want to be at B House, why not go to a hotel? There's a Grand in town, you know, two, at least. And, you have a bunch of friends who'd walk through fire for you. Are you telling me none of them would take you in?"

"I didn't ask."

"If you wanted to be free of everything Breckenridge—why would you want to be free of everything Breckenridge? You love your family. I love your family. Your family are amazing. And if you say any different, I'll know this is some government cover-up, a high-level conspiracy. If Xavien Rourke has roped you into something—what's going on?"

"You never answered on the drink," he said, strolling to the kitchen. Such slow, lithe movement, his purpose was sure, though not betrayed in the certainty of his gait. "Still off alcohol?"

"It's barely dinnertime. Is that what you do now? Spend your days drinking? Hell of a long time to conceal a habit."

"Are you hungry?"

It was like she wasn't speaking at all. Did he have his hearing off?

"You want to take me out to dinner?" With him in sweats and a tee-shirt, nothing on his feet, he was hardly ready for their usual haunts. "Too bad, I don't date crazy people." Or ignorant ones, which seemed to be his current persona. "We're not going out before we talk about this. Ignore me as long as you like, Stat, I'll just keep asking. Have you forgotten I can be persistent? I get what I want, Breckenridge."

From him anyway. Usually.

"Talk about what?"

Like it was—this guy. "Why did you quit? Spell it out for me because I'm absolutely… flummoxed. This is not the Breck I know. Why?"

"Because I'm done."

"Done?"

"The other night…" He produced two bottles of water from the fridge. "Zairn and I talked. Our conversation put some things in perspective."

"How is that an answer to—what did he put in your head? Are you telling me to ask him your reasons? I will. Don't think I won't. I'll go right over there and—"

"Nothing is more important to me than you. Nothing." Wha—what? Was that a…? What were they talking about now? Was this another subject change? "Life is simple when love's involved. You decide how much you want it. What you're willing to sacrifice."

And she didn't get it. "Who asked you to sacrifice?"

"I don't know why I didn't see it. Being together is an option; it's always an option."

"That's what Zairn told you? He's not a guy you've ever aspired to be. I love Zairn, you know that, but you're very different men. His life is not your life."

"No, he found clarity long before I did. He wouldn't take my bullshit and was right to call me on it, to make me face it." He came to hand her one of the bottles of water. "What's worth most to you, that's what your life's about. Time is finite."

"Your mortality? That's what this is about."

"Zairn's in love. Him and Roxie, it's what his life's about, and that wasn't an easy path. Didn't matter; he owns his choice, doesn't doubt for a second it was the right one."

"You think we've chosen an easy path?"

"I think it's about time we both got our shit together."

She tossed the water onto the couch too. "Speak for yourself, my shit is fine."

Before that morning, she'd have said his was better. Showed what she knew, and how quickly things could change.

"You're right. This is about me. My choices."

"You don't suddenly choose to abandon your family. Something else is going on here."

He twisted the cap from his bottle and took a long slow drink, never breaking eye contact, not even after he lowered it.

"Something that should've happened long ago. Coy, this is my decision. It's one I hope you'll support. My family are confused too..." He exhaled a snicker and sipped some more water. "Which is funny, because life has never been so clear to me."

"And this is it, what you choose? To sleep on your brother's couch, hang out all day alone? This is better than working with your family? With me?" She got a little closer. "If this is about me, do you need me to leave? To quit Breckenridge? If one of us needs to step aside, it has to be me. Why wouldn't you just—"

"No, I need you at Breckenridge," he said. "For now anyway. In the future, we can decide—"

"Stat," she said, taking his hand to reverse to the

couch and sit down. This wasn't working, whatever he was thinking, it wasn't translating. "Tell me the plan. What's the plan?"

He sat, putting his bottle on the coffee table to gather her other hand into his too. "First, I have to get a job."

"You had a job. Breckenridge is your job. More than a job. Why—"

"I need something unconnected to the family. Something unconnected to anyone we care about."

Which immediately excluded Rouge, Crimson's parent company, the Grand Hotel chain, and CollCom, all places that would hire him in a heartbeat. Truth was, when the world at large heard Rankin Breckenridge was job hunting, he'd be inundated with offers. Still didn't explain his actions.

"Why?" she asked again like it was becoming her catchphrase. "Why avoid the people we care about? Is this some deluded notion about making it on your own? Because you earned your spot. It's not nepotism." Not only nepotism. "You're amazing at what you do."

"No, this isn't about ego. You know me better than that." Did she? Because she hadn't seen this coming, had never even entertained the notion. "I'll have to take a pay cut; I've already relinquished my trust and frozen my bank accounts."

Though her lips puckered, ready to ask the question again, they stalled. He hadn't just quit his job and left the family home, he was shunning the fortune too. Money he'd earned in addition to the fortune he'd been bestowed. Rather than enlighten her, everything he said only served to confuse the situation even more.

"I don't understand."

Being a man who exhibited infinite patience and care, he'd never taunt her ignorance, she did wish he'd satisfy it though.

"This is what I choose. You are what I choose." When her head shook, he tightened his hold on her hands. "I promise you I'll find employment. I will find somewhere for us to live. I will build us a life that no one can take advantage of."

Ah, and suddenly, all became clear. "This is about my dad. Goddamnit." Throwing his hands back, she shot to her feet. "The man is a thousand miles away and he still comes between us."

"I should've heard you. From the beginning. We might not have a billion-dollar lifestyle, but we'll be free. Money means nothing. We can be together."

"So what? You think this fixes everything? You think this is what I wanted? I love your family; you love your family."

"We can still love them without working for them."

"This isn't right. Don't you see? This is exactly what I was worried about. You're giving him power over us."

"No. I'm taking that power back. Being together is an option. And if, for that to happen, you need me to insulate my family from what yours might do to them, that's exactly what I'll do. I'll have no influence, I'll have no sway. Regardless of whatever your father asks—"

"I don't want him to cause a rift. It's wrong."

"I won't work for people we care about. I won't earn enough to flag on his radar. If we have nothing to offer him, he'll leave us alone. That's what you always wanted, for us to have a life together that can't be infiltrated by him. I'll give it to you, Coy, just give me a little time."

"How can you think—you really think you can do this?"

"It'll take time."

"And in the meantime? I just wait around until

you make it all better?"

She so wasn't that woman.

"I'll wait," he said. "I won't ask you to do the same."

Zairn damn Lomond had a lot to answer for. He shouldn't go around putting ideas in people's heads. What? Because things were all roses for him and Roxie, somehow, he believed that should make things roses for everyone? Life wasn't like that.

"Go back to Breckenridge."

"No."

"Go back to the house at least, it isn't right for you to be here like this."

"I've made up my mind, Coy."

And that stern attitude betrayed his adamance. Great. This train was on the tracks. How long before it wrecked?

This was surreal. "You're sleeping on your brother's couch."

"It pulls out."

Oh, and that made all the difference?

"You're being a regular joe, not taking advantage of the generosity of those who care about you…" Which was funny given how generous he, and all the Breckenridges were. "You're playing this like you know no one, like you don't have access to what you have access to."

"I don't need access to do this right. Darroch and Savvy don't mind me being here, they stay at B House too. They have space anywhere they need it."

Support not judgment. Oh, Breckenridge.

"Regardless, you can't kick them out of their place." She exhaled and swiped up her purse. "You still have a key to my apartment. Use it. Stay there."

"Coy, I won't rush you—"

"Yeah, you're not getting any, don't even think

about that. I have a second bedroom." That she had designs on turning into a nursery. With those ideas on hold, there was no reason he shouldn't use it. "And don't go telling people we live together. It's temporary."

She got two steps before he snagged her wrist to halt her. "Where are you going?"

"To the source," she said, as fueled by urgency then as she had been on arriving, though for different reasons. "To do something I should've done a thousand times already."

ELEVEN

HOW LONG HAD SHE known Zairn Lomond? A long time. They'd never been close, yet that wouldn't stop her giving him both barrels. What was he thinking of putting ideas in Breck's head? Yeah, okay, so Breck wasn't usually easily led, in fact, some may call him a cynic, a skeptical cynic, but this U-turn was way out of character.

If Zairn had the idea she was some wallflower, he was about to learn otherwise. Breck wanted to take action? She'd take action. Damn right. Get her shit together? Her shit was about to be collated quick smart.

Returning to Rouge HQ, the scene of the crime, so to speak, the elevator granted her access to the executive floor where security guards spotted her. Crossing the floor's lobby, she called a different elevator, one with intricate engravings, different from the others: Zairn's private elevator.

Her clearance wouldn't get her any higher, no, but she'd made a call. Not to the Rouge Overlord himself, nope, why give the guy notice of her wrath? No.

Calm down. That wasn't the way to think about it. This impromptu meeting couldn't be adversarial. They should be allies. Fat chance of that if he matched her attitude.

She should've got rid of her fizzing energy before rocking up there. Another bad idea, she was on a role. The available outlet for depressurization before the journey over was Breck... and an empty apartment. And, oh, yeah, that guy was plenty good at diverting and expending her energy. Nope. Nope. Bad. Bad plan. She wasn't sleeping with him again until he'd got *his* shit together. And the shit she meant wasn't close to what he meant.

What had she been thinking telling him to go to her apartment? Yes, it made more sense for him to have his own room than to take up residence in his brother's girlfriend's miniscule loft. Not that it was embarrassingly miniscule—it was palatial in Manhattan terms at the estimated price point—but way too small to hold two Breckenridges.

It wasn't like she and Breck had never lived together before, they had on and off for years, though it was "unofficial." It wouldn't surprise her if Darroch and Savvy's living arrangement was unofficial too, regardless of their engagement. Alice Breckenridge liked to think of all her boys living at home and no one refuted that.

Breck knew her apartment and to treat it as his own. As a roommate, he'd be conscientious, neat, respectful... A roommate? No, they'd never done that. Could they be roomies?

Another alien concept.

The elevator opened, producing Tripp. Ah, thank goodness, her ticket up.

"Seq..."

Laying her hands on his chest, she advanced, reversing him back into the elevator. "I need to go upstairs, Priest. All the way to the top."

"Yeah," he said, pressing a button that closed the doors. "You said on the phone. What's so urgent? Want to fill me in?"

"I don't have clearance to get into Zairn's penthouse."

"Not many people do."

Reaching up, she ran her hand through his mussed hair in a pointless attempt at taming it. God, lovable rogue was so effortless.

"Ever heard of a comb?" She tucked a stray section behind his ear and smoothed his stubble. "This is the end of the day for most people. Did you just wake up?"

"Wake up? No. Get out of bed…"

Her hands dropped. "Please tell me you showered."

"I showered," he said, though his proceeding smirk contradicted the words. "I did…" then came a mutter, "just wasn't the one holding the soap."

With a head bob to the side and a brow flick, he disarmed everyone within a twelve-block radius.

"Okay, you get me inside and then you can go back to your lady… or ladies. I don't want to know anything you wouldn't tell your mother."

Reaching past her, he hit a button. "Are you sure anyone's in the penthouse?"

"It's as good a place as any to start looking."

"You're amped," Tripp said. "Cabe said you went to find Breck. Any movement?"

"Not yet," she said, restraining a growl though there was no doubt her pseudo-brother-in-law didn't see the truth of it in her expression. "I'm working on it."

"It's always you, Seq," he said, draping an arm around her. "You're his world."

"That's never felt more like an accusation." Not because of his tone, he was ever-and-always charming

Tripp, non-judgmental, accepting, relaxed. Her own conscience on the other hand… "I'll put this back together."

"Got a plan?"

She bit the corner of her lip. "I'm working on that too."

Thankful for the interruption, the moment they arrived at their destination, she was out on the hunt. Her first target wasn't far away. The person in the living room leaped to their feet, but it wasn't the somebody she was looking for.

"Roxie," she said on a rush of breath, looking left and right. "I need Zairn."

"He's not here." Roxie's concern slowed her heart a little. "He's at a meeting downtown. What do you need? I have access to pretty much everything—no, make that everything Zairn does."

Tripp eased into her peripheral vision, slipping his hands in his pockets. "Seq…?"

Her gaze trailed to him. "If you want to leave, now is the time to go, because the shutters are about to come down. This is eyes only."

"When have you known me to shy from trouble?"

She couldn't blame him for figuring there would be trouble. It was in her heritage. In her blood. She was the Jekyll and Hyde character in a cartoon, perfectly normal looking and amiable, while trailing around a cloud of thunder and lightning, zapping the poor people caught in her wake. Ha, if that was her, imagine what followed her father.

"We need to talk about my sister."

Though her focus was back on Roxie, Tripp's fingers threaded between hers, locking them in support and comfort. And, no, she wasn't thinking about what may have occupied those hands not so long ago.

"Your sister?" Roxie said, folding her arms in sync with a quick, shallow head shake. "Okay, has he spoken to her recently?"

"I don't know. I need to know where she is. He's the only one who knows." The only one she knew who knew. "Unless he told you."

Would her newly minted friend trust her enough to reveal the answer? She wasn't sure she wanted Roxie to surrender too fast. Yes, she needed to know, but she also didn't want her sister's location given up too easy.

And what a can of worms. Okay, she admitted it, she'd avoided Zairn for this precise reason. Not that their paths crossed often, but, until recently, she'd never actively swerved him. Actively might be a bit much, except... When she heard what happened, heard there was a plan in the works, the first thing she should've done was get on board and track Zairn down. Instead, she poured wine and went for a soak in the tub.

No amount of scrubbing would ever get that stink off.

"I'm behind the curve here," Roxie said, glancing at Tripp. How could she be confused when the truth was so dire? Maybe the woman wasn't sharp after all. "I'm looking for a Drury sister? Don't think I know a Drury sister..."

Oh, shit. Duh. That explained the confusion.

"Seq uses her mom's maiden name," Tripp explained. "You're not looking for a Drury."

Perhaps for dramatic effect, he lingered. She could speak up, should speak up; it had been so long since she'd confessed the truth out loud. Confessed her shame. Owned her lineage. In her defense, it was a lineage she didn't want. Couldn't pick your family, right?

Maybe that's what it was, Tripp wasn't pausing to build the tension, he'd presented an opening he expected her to seize. Right, cue taken, time for her line...

"Still none the wiser..." Roxie might be chill now, how would she feel after hearing the truth? God, she hated when new people found out. The questions. Intrigue. Assumptions. Judgment. "I can snake Z's phone if we take a ride. Whoever she is, she'll be in there."

"She won't." Her mouth dried, but this was it, no out now. "He wouldn't be that careless."

And knowing Zairn, not everyone in his directory would be listed under their real name. She'd be surprised if he even used his regular phone when talking to her sister.

Roxie's aura thickened. "This is serious."

"I'll say," Tripp said and picked up her missed line. "Seq here's a Gambatto."

"A Gamba—"

Roxie may have stopped talking, but her mouth stayed open.

"Yes, I confess," she said on a resigned sigh. Where was that energy when she needed it? "My father is one of the nation's biggest crime bosses—was. That's obviously changed in recent—since everything. I hear the Irish have it now."

Roxie's arms fell loose at her sides, swinging under their own momentum. "You're from Chicago?" Wait... what? "Oh my God!" Roxie hurried over to pull her into a hug. "How in the hell have you been in this city so long and we haven't found each other?"

When the woman drew back, huge smile on her face, Sequoia almost recoiled. This was not a typical reaction to the news.

"From—yes—yes, I'm from Chicago."

"You hide it well, why do you hide it? I should've known with the deep dish. Damn me for being distracted by its deliciousness. I saw you loved it, I just thought you had great taste."

"I don't—"

"Oh my God!" Roxie hugged her again. "I will never forgive Zairn for hiding this from me."

"I don't think he would hide it—"

"He definitely hid it," Tripp said, all mischief.

Roxie took her hand and led her to the couch. She didn't let go of Tripp, so he came too.

"This is perfect, amazing, I need more of home here. Do you get back much?"

"I don't get back at all." Talk about active avoidance? "I won't go within a hundred miles of the city. Of the state."

"Because you and your dad…" As Roxie trailed off, all three of them sat down. "Your sister. Trish? You want to talk to Trish?"

"Yes. I need to know where she is."

"Because you want to…"

"Hear her testimony. I need to know how this will play out. Is it Joey? Is it Dad? What is she giving up because there are a lot of skeletons…"

"I imagine there'd have to be. Plan to talk her out of it?"

"No! Definitely no. That's her choice. A brave one, but…"

"Easier with someone like Zairn stacking the deck," Roxie said, then dropped a bomb. "He won't tell you."

That honesty startled her. "He won't—"

"He won't tell anyone."

"No one?" Tripp asked. "He's told no one?"

"Kinloch, in case he drops down dead, but anyone looking for Trish would have to find Mr. Gramercy-Peake first. Good luck to them. If they find him, they'd almost deserve the answer just as a reward for the achievement."

"I need to talk to my sister."

"Why the sudden urgency?" Roxie asked. "She's been off the grid for—"

"Zairn and I don't talk much, but I trust him to take the situation seriously."

"He does. He absolutely does. She's safe, you don't have to worry about that. Although…"

"Although what?" Was this going to be a fight? If Roxie stood in her way, Zairn would never budge. "She's my sister. I love her."

"And rocking up to her door could draw the kind of attention we don't want."

Would a phone call be enough? She couldn't deny the idea of seeing her sister again was appealing. It had been so long, *so* long, since she'd been face to face with any Gambatto other than herself. Sometimes it was difficult to look in the mirror for that very reason.

"She's the only one I can trust. Trish won't lie to me."

"Maybe not…" Roxie said, clucking her tongue.

"You sure about that?" Tripp asked. "It's been a long time…"

"Yes, it has, but—"

"Okay," Roxie interrupted and bounced to her feet. "I've got this."

"You'll call Zairn?"

"Nope. I'll call Dennis."

The woman dashed to grab a phone from an end table near the fireplace.

"Dennis?" she asked, casting her eyes to Tripp.

"Her pilot." Tripp's intrigue-laced words closed around her. "Where we going, Rox Out?"

Phone still at her ear, Roxie tipped her chin toward them, showing a broad smile. "Home."

TWELVE

"I'VE BEEN ON PRIVATE planes, but, wow," she said, more impressed by what was inside than the clouds or the country beneath.

A chessboard, a fireplace, thick carpets and mood lighting, this was no ordinary airplane.

"Puts the rest of us to shame, doesn't it?" Tripp asked, reclining his chair to lay flat. "Z has class, Rox Out."

"Yeah. Me. I'm his class." Roxie shook up their cocktails in the mixer. "Welcome to the Zee-Jet, Sequoia, yet another jewel in our Crimson crown. Very top-secret, exclusive clientele only. Not for public consumption. I thought the Crimson Craft would be overkill for three passengers. It's a Triple Seven. And I hear it's being decked out for the wedding anyway."

"I should get me one of these," Tripp said, adjusting his shoulders. "About time I had my own wings."

"The amount you travel, I'm surprised you don't."

"He's the only freeloading billionaire you'll ever meet," Roxie said. "He doesn't actually own anything, just sponges off the rest of us."

"Watching those interest digits roll over and over on the trust fund account day after day, Rox Out. Waiting to sweep the table."

"Don't wait too long or all my single friends will be taken," Roxie said. "You know, the day you take a woman home to your mother, she'll fall to her knees and kiss the floor. She needs to know you'll be looked after because, let's be honest, you can't look after yourself."

"How'd we get from money to women?"

Roxie arched a brow at him. "One is more valuable than the other."

"Tell Brant, boy's still a virgin, but knows the market better than any other guy I ever met."

"And whose fault is that?" Roxie asked. "You have a massive surplus of women and you've never taken pity on your little brother? One of your harem must owe you a favor—consensually, of course. And you know almost every female on the planet, are you saying there's none compatible with him? No chance any woman would be attracted to him? He's cute."

"I love the guy, he's my brother."

"You just can't stand him."

"Doesn't feel right to lumber any woman with him, even for a night."

"So tie him up and gag him, he doesn't have to talk to her."

"Window into your relationship there?" Tripp teased. "Always wondered how Zairn did it night after night."

Speaking of the man... "Was Zairn okay with you leaving town, Roxie?"

Hard to believe he could be if Roxie was honest about their purpose. Maybe he'd be okay with it, if he was present. How had Roxie kept him away and stolen his plane? Woman was impressive.

Tripp stretched out, closing his eyes and locking his hands on top of his head. "She hasn't called him."

"I'll get around to it."

"As soon as she finds a charger for her phone."

"Yeah? Laugh it up, Playboy Junior. Have you called your mom?"

"My mom knows better than to assume I'll be on any one continent for any length of time. As long as I'm on the planet, she's good."

"Just follow the pretty girls, don't you, Priest?"

"No, Rox Out, they follow me. Haven't figured that out yet?"

"That's right, I forgot, you're Zairn's redirect."

"Haven't returned one to sender yet. You maintain the supply and I'll deliver on their demands."

Their easy rapport would have more of an impact, if she wasn't painfully aware of how impulsive decisions could backfire. Normally, that would be okay, kind of, like when she and Breck broke their invisible, though spoken, boundaries. That was more okay than where they were heading. Why wasn't she better at thinking things through?

"My father will know I'm in town."

Better to warn them of what may await than be faced with the Great Gambatto without warning. Who was she kidding? Her father wouldn't show up himself, even now, while bottoming out, he'd believe it beneath him. Didn't mean she wouldn't be summoned.

"You think he'll track you down?"

"My security guys will handle it," Roxie said, pouring bright liquid into martini glasses. "They're professionals. They can handle anything."

"Handle my father? Do you know he comes with goons and guns?"

And absolute entitlement drizzled in arrogant superiority.

The question was rhetorical.

Tripp snickered. "A shootout, a showdown, boy, am I glad I came."

"No one asked you to come, Priest," Roxie said, coming over to hand her a glass. "You're a curtain-twitcher."

"Never miss a chance to twitch."

"No, you don't. Certain parts of you anyway. Oh, and I meant to say, there's a shower back there, if you want to wash Natie off," Roxie said. "Was it Natie? Her cousin? Her sister? Best friend? All of the above? I lost track last night."

"He told me he showered after sex," she said, enjoying how Tripp cracked open an eye just as Roxie waved the glass in front of him.

"I'm sure he did," Roxie said. Sitting up, Tripp took the glass. "But they tend to cry and cling when he tells them he's leaving town. Lots of tears and boogers."

"Can't help that I'm irresistible. She'll wait," Tripp said, sipping the drink, then scowling at it. "What is this?"

"Virgin."

After the explanation, Roxie spun on the spot to sashay back to the bar, serving admirable class with that sass.

"Been a while since I had one of those," Tripp said, swallowing some more. "Tastes good."

"Oh, please, you could line them up."

"Don't have to, Z does that for me every birthday."

"So that's what the auditions were for..." Roxie teased. "If we're going to make a Breckenridge baby, Seq has to keep that system tiptop. So. Virgin."

"Gotta make my mother proud of me," Tripp

muttered.

Usually, she was all about the banter. Nothing better than hanging out with positive people, enjoying each other, fun, frolics—did they forget where the plane intended to land?

"I must be drunk on something to be heading back home," she said, wishing for liquor… or maybe a tranquilizer. "I can't believe Zairn would set Trish up so close to our father. Do you know the breadth of his contacts? I'm surprised he hasn't found her already."

"Oh, we're not going to see Trish. I don't know where she is. No idea." Roxie sank into her seat with a flourish. "Not a clue and I don't plan to ask."

"But I thought…"

"You want answers? Answers are what you'll get. I know who can give them. Honest and true. No danger or jeopardy required."

"Who?"

Smiling again, Roxie's shoulders pushed back into the lush leather. "Trust me. I've got this."

"Someone in Chicago?"

Her father wouldn't allow two betrayers to keep breathing. At least her sister was blood, that might earn her the right to keep her life, *might*, that wasn't close to guaranteed. Anyone else turning on him would get short shrift. They'd be lucky if they saw it coming. Goodbyes? Apologies? Mercy…? Ha! Not a damn chance.

"Yep," Roxie said. "Z and your father aren't the only ones with contacts." Her friend crossed her legs and leaned closer. "Did you tell Breck we were leaving New York?"

"She hasn't called him either. Not great communicators you pair."

Mr. Tripp Know-It-All Breckenridge, she hadn't confessed the omission, it was just coincidence he was right. Coincidence. Sigh, no, Tripp knew women.

Somehow, despite growing up surrounded by males, he held the key to the female psyche.

"He'd want to be here and that's exactly what I don't want," she said. "I don't want my father anywhere near him, near anything Breckenridge."

With her glass, Roxie gestured at their travel companion. "We'll dress him up in disguise. He can be our groupie."

"Not so easy to hide this magnificence, baby."

"We'll tell him you're our gigolo on hand."

"Then you better call your boyfriend, Rox Out, 'cause the press will eat that shit up."

"My father doesn't like the press."

"I bet he doesn't," Roxie said. "You think Breck wouldn't support you? Is that the problem? 'Cause Tripp will kick his ass if—"

"Of course he'd support me. Which is exactly why I said the shutters were down." She set her certainty on Tripp. "No one is to know where we are or what we're doing."

"Wouldn't worry too much," Tripp said. "Breck's done the whole renounce his trust thing. Dude's pauper poor and wouldn't take a cent from the rest of us. How's he supposed to get here with no doubloons?"

Wouldn't matter to Breck. Even if he had to walk to get to her, he wouldn't hesitate.

"This is a problem I'm fixing on my own. Your brother is not allowed near this tarpit. Please, I need this kept quiet."

If for no other reason, the more people in the circle, the more people her father could hurt.

"Don't have to tell me twice. Your secrets are my secrets." And everyone got that courtesy, those who knew him, complete strangers too, hence why he was also known as Priest. "What's the plan?" Tripp asked, finishing his drink and getting up to take the glass back to the bar. "Why does Trish's testimony matter now? Didn't matter last week, last month."

It did, it should've, if she'd been more diligent. Yes, she'd been complacent but had reasons for burying her head in the sand. She knew that world, the one she'd abandoned, that life, and didn't need anyone to deliver the grimy details. Until then. Revisiting it may not be number one on her to-do list, but lovely, wonderful Breck had forced her hand. Maybe not on purpose, man had a way of adjusting her focus without even trying.

Still, Tripp's query was valid and he deserved an honest answer. "Because if all she plans to do is send my brother to prison for murdering Ava, there's a chance of my father clawing his way back to the top." Or at least regaining enough stability to return to his interfering ways. Worse than that, he'd need a major investment to do it. And who did they know with money…? Not happening. "Dad can do it without Joey."

"There's been a lot of scrutiny."

"By the media and law enforcement alike. No one's missing this chance."

"You included," Tripp said. "You've got to get in while the going's good."

"You love him," Roxie said, attracting her attention. "It doesn't matter what anyone else is saying, or where anyone else is, you love Breck."

"Yes." She exhaled. "But life isn't that easy."

"It is." Roxie's smile told a story of its own. "You think it was easy for me to admit that? It took me a minute, but it's true. You just make the decision to be together and let everything else go to hell."

"Yes, that sounds mighty similar to the speech my guy got from yours last week."

"That's what this is about?" Tripp asked, downing a shot of something clear. "That's why Breck quit the company? Z told him to?"

"I doubt he said it like that, but this whole mess was prompted by some conversation they had that night."

"Huh," Tripp said, downing another shot. "Explains why they were stuck in their little huddle for so long."

And if only she'd known about that at the time. Though what would she have done? Put herself between them. It probably wouldn't be the best moment to make the point that simply by showing up, she could sway Breck.

"It's romantic to think love can overcome everything," she said, appealing to Roxie. "But unrealistic. If something in your life hurt Zairn just because you were together, would you put him through that or cut him loose to protect him?"

"Zairn wouldn't put up with that," Roxie said, "didn't put up with it. I'm willing to bet Breck's of the same ilk."

"He's a stubborn sonofabitch," Tripp added.

"Wonder where he gets that from."

"Breckenridges are raised to be relentless." But not cutthroat. They were the kindest persistent people anyone would ever meet. "You really want to stop him, Seq? 'Cause there's an easy way to do it."

Quit? Cut ties? Tell him they would never happen? That last one would have to be delivered just right or he'd never believe it. They'd said it so many times and still didn't manage to stay away from each other.

"He told me why he's doing this." For her. "This isn't my attempt to stop him. It's my attempt to get a final definitive answer once and for all."

Was she with him or walking away?

After learning about her father's potential fate, she'd know if there was a chance. The Gambatto empire had been slowly collapsing since the debacle began, her father wasn't as powerful as he once was. If the law put him away for good, the threat wouldn't be gone, but it would be minimized.

Was there a chance they could be together if that happened? She wouldn't get her hopes up or anyone else's either.

THIRTEEN

A CAR WAITED for them on the tarmac after they landed. She didn't know where they were going, a hotel, she guessed.

Wrongly.

When they stopped, they were outside a pretty standard, non-descript building on a residential street. Nothing fancy, nothing spectacular, not a typical Billionaire's Row. Huh, interesting.

"Welcome home!" the guy who'd opened the car door beamed at Roxie. "Where the hell have you been?"

"I got a little lost," Roxie said, hugging the guy. "What did I miss?"

"So much."

"I'll bet." Roxie touched his face. "It's good to see you, Trevor. Did His Majesty call?"

"Might've."

"Mm."

"You should call him."

"I'll get around to it," Roxie said and gestured at them. "Trevor, you remember Tripp. And this is

Sequoia. We're protecting her from the mafia."

"Cool," Trevor said. "Just like any other Friday."

Her friend leaned in to murmur. "Told you he was good."

"Whatever you need."

"I need to get off the street before—"

Roxie stopped when a guy jumped out from somewhere.

Where?

From nowhere. Where the hell did he come from? Was he hiding behind Trevor?

Without even turning around, Trevor's arm shot out to block the guy from getting too close.

"Roxie!" the surprise guy called. "Rox, where's Zairn? What happened? Are you fighting? Are you over? Are you calling off the wedding?"

"I missed you too, Mr. Lurker. You're just so much more endearing than the masses of your colleagues that surround our New York home on a daily basis."

Sarcasm could be a useful tool.

"Rox—"

"Zairn is fine, I am fine, and everything is on track for the wedding of the century."

As her friend whirled to flounce away, the surprise guy blinked, frozen in what appeared to be shock.

Tripp draped an arm around her. "She doesn't usually talk to him so much."

Guided up the stairs and through a communal entrance into a stairway, she wasn't exactly sure why they were there. What an odd place to—unless it was a secret residence. Not so secret if that guy outside was from the press.

People in her father's line of work had secret safe houses, maybe Zairn and Roxie did too.

Roxie walked down a particular hallway, through

a specific door, and threw her arms out wide, tossing her head back to breathe in deep.

"God, it feels good to be home."

Home? Home! This was Roxie's home.

Scanning the space, a smile grew slowly. An apartment, furnished, a kitchen with appliances, nothing too shiny or new, lived in, this was Roxie's apartment. Even after getting with Zairn, they'd kept it.

"This is where you live?"

"Where she lived with Toria and Jane before meeting Zairn," Tripp said, retreating to the kitchen as she and Roxie went deeper inside.

"And you still own it?"

"I don't own it," Roxie said, kicking off her shoes and pulling out her hair clip to toss it over the back of the couch onto the seat.

"You rent?"

"No, we don't pay for it," Roxie said then hummed. "I don't think."

"So it belongs to someone else?"

"Belongs…? No. We don't care about that shit in our group. Now! Before we do anything else—"

"Roxie!"

Spinning around, seeking the source of the exclamation, a short beauty rushed through the front door prompting Roxie to meet her with exuberance.

"Rainie!" The women embraced. "My dear, sweet Rainie. How have you been, beautiful? Where's Gauge?"

"At the office—when is he not, huh?"

"Oh, honey, I'm sorry. You want me to go over there and drag him back here? Sometimes they need a little snapback to reality."

"Oh, no, he works out of the office upstairs. One of the apartments has become a sort of satellite division for… well, everything. It's all corporate up there now."

"I heard you set up home across the hall."

"We did and go in and out of Viva when we need to—oh, who cares about that? You brought friends!"

"I did." Arms still around each other, the women turned to them. "Sequoia Drury, this is Rainie Tait, a very good friend. And—"

"Tripp Breckenridge," he introduced himself.

Rainie's head tilted. "Are you hitting on me?"

"Sure. If you want me to hit on you."

"Your name," Roxie said. "That's all you have to say."

He shrugged. "Sometimes I don't even have to say that." Approaching, he bobbed his chin. "You broke Demetri Lozano's heart."

Rainie inhaled, but quickly sealed her lips, her startled eyes blinking. "You know Dem?"

"Tripp knows everyone," Roxie said. "Is Gwenie living at yours or here?"

"Downstairs," Rainie said. "Next door to Porter."

"Next—next to—excuse me?" Obviously, Roxie hadn't expected to hear that name. "Porter lives in the building now? Our building? My building?"

"There's full-time security here, which is good given... everything... No one but our people so much as set foot on the stoop," Rainie said. "He said it was a temporary thing, but it's nice having him around. He's a great guy; killer when we crack out the Trivial Pursuit."

"Yes, he is, when he's not being an idiot and trying to get himself killed," Roxie said and drew in a breath so deep, her shoulders rose. "Huh, okay, I suppose this works out better. Perfect." Roxie started to move but swung back around. "Z knew about this? About Porter being in residence?"

"They talk a lot." Rainie wasn't shy about sharing. "Alex likes him too."

"Oh, good, so long as Gauge likes him." Roxie growled. "Someone won't be getting laid any time soon."

"Zairn's in a different state," Tripp said, retrieving wine from the fridge to go with the glasses he'd found somewhere. "Makes it more difficult."

"Whose side are you on?"

"Porter?" Sequoia said, interrupting the flow. "Who is Porter?"

"Clement." Roxie extended an arm her way, opening and closing her hand. "Come meet him."

"Why do I want to meet him?"

Roxie hadn't immediately said anything about meeting Gauge or any of the other people they talked about. Why was this Porter different? It was late, she'd worked all day, was she capable of making a good first impression? Should she care?

"Trust me," Roxie said, waiting for her to go over and join their hands. "You want to meet him." Their hostess switched to Tripp. "You coming?"

"Sure," Tripp said, putting the wine back in the fridge, corkscrew and all. "Never miss a chance to get the gory details." He joined them and slipped his hand into her free one. "Should be interesting."

"I'll order supplies for tonight," Rainie called when the door opened. "But don't make plans for tomorrow, we're going to the club. I have so much to show you!"

The club? What club? Whichever club it was became less important as they traipsed down the hallway.

"We going to the club tonight?"

"Obviously not," Roxie said in answer to Tripp's question. "Hence why Rainie said tomorrow. This is the woman's purpose, let her be."

"I'd rather just order food and get some sleep," Sequoia chimed in. "We're in the perfect place for deep dish." Nothing. She wasn't the only one caught up in her own head. "Anyone?"

Her brother-in-law paid her no heed. "Rox Out, we live to party. You have the means to make it happen…"

His singsong cajoling didn't change their hostess' mind. "You won't die if you don't blast your eardrums and get laid every night, Priest."

"Maybe. I don't know. You're up there with me, babe. How do you know this isn't the end for both of us?"

"Because I can go without for one night."

"Music maybe. You're only saying the other thing 'cause your guy's in a different state. That shouldn't mean we're all deprived."

"You had sex already today, and besides, I don't care if you get laid. Go find someone to screw. Have at her. Just meet Porter first and take Trevor with you if you go out. Your mom would never forgive me for abandoning one of her babies in a strange, but fabulous, city."

They descended a floor.

"She has a lot of babies," Tripp said. "Might not notice."

No chance. Alice may care about a lot of people, but there was no way she'd be okay with losing track of one of her boys, even at Tripp's age… or Breck's.

"We're all her babies, and she may be taking on more from what I hear."

"More? What do you know that I don't?"

Unusual for Tripp to be out of the loop.

Roxie stopped at the head of the hall. "That will have to wait."

"Rox—"

"Porter!"

The sudden shout startled her, though maybe it shouldn't have. They hadn't been told exactly which apartment belonged to this Porter. Belonged? If he didn't pay rent either, "housed" would be a better description. Imagine how the price of real estate in the area must've skyrocketed given it had become a billionaire's hangout.

"You're subtle, Rox Out," Tripp said, letting go to stretch. "We could just start knocking. Are the doors even locked? There's security swarming all over the place here, can't tell me the main door isn't guarded too. How many people live here?"

Roxie looped her and Sequoia's arms together to get closer. "See he's trying misdirection, pretending like he forgot someone said a single female lives on this floor too."

His smile came first, then the bob of his brows. "No harm in being neighborly. It's how my momma raised me."

"Yeah, Breckenridge House doesn't have neighbors, not for like a mile."

"We took long walks as children."

"Mm, yeah," Roxie said, her scrutiny growing. "You're not usually so actively horny this early. What's going on?"

FOURTEEN

THERE WAS NO TIME to answer because the nearest door opened, and a guy popped his head out. He blinked once, then came out to fold his arms.

"RoRo. This is a surprise. Z didn't tell me you were coming."

"What is with Casanova buddying up to the men in my life?"

"Am I in your life?"

Fully entitled, Roxie marched on over and shoved his door further open. "We have to talk."

"We?" he asked, then landed his focus on her and Tripp. "Or all of we?" With a quick arm jab, Roxie wrung a snicker from Porter who went inside, gesturing for them to follow. "Come on in."

"Great place you've got here," Roxie said, opening her arms to turn on the spot.

Filled with Porter's things, not Roxie's, obviously, the furniture was laid out differently, but, yeah, from what she saw, one apartment had the same footprint as the other.

"Didn't think you'd have a problem with it. Z thought you'd prefer me somewhere safe and the Grand isn't exactly home."

That was a matter of opinion.

"I don't have a problem," Roxie admitted. "But I draw the line at the magician. He shows up looking for a place to live, you and Z just turn him right around."

"The magician?" Tripp asked, clearly amused.

Porter explained. "An ex."

"Not one I care about being safe." Roxie's compliment softened Porter's smile. In typical fashion, Roxie pulled the sentimentality back fast. "Though I wouldn't have to think about your safety if you didn't make dumb, suicidal career decisions."

"Still on that?"

"Why is it you needed a new place to live?" Roxie asked, tapping a straight forefinger on her jaw. "Oh, that's right, because your last place got torched."

"Now I have round the clock security."

"*I* have round the clock security." Roxie's manicured middle finger touched her breast. "You're taking advantage of it."

"You're not here to use it!" Porter laughed. "And don't you have a security team in New York too?"

Somehow, she figured, he knew the answer to that question.

"I'm moving on." Roxie hitched her chin. "What you got to drink in this joint?"

Like the words were a command for Tripp, he swung the door closed and drifted into the kitchen to begin the hunt.

"Didn't think I'd see you before the wedding," Porter said, smirking. "Second thoughts? Come here for one last hurrah?"

Roxie's shoulders dropped. "Yes, Porter, I'm here to beg you to take me back. Want to run away together?"

"Might be hard with the guy you're jilting owning his own jets."

"And the building you're standing in," Tripp muttered, landing on vodka in the freezer. "Oh, this is good stuff."

"Help yourself." Wasn't exactly clear if Porter was sincere or not. "You're not one of her usual girls."

"Yeah, given the penis and all." Roxie went toward the desk in the corner. The huge desk, covered with papers, bearing an open laptop. "Tripp's an honorary girl."

"Tripp…" Porter whipped around fast. "Wait, you're not—you are."

"A Breckenridge?" Roxie asked, twirling into the tall desk chair. "Yeah, so he can afford to replace the liquor… 'can' but probably won't. Bill Z for it."

"Tripp Breckenridge." Porter shook a pointed finger at him. "You're number seven."

"In the line of succession?" Tripp was still investigating the kitchen. "I'm somewhere around there. Impressive. You a groupie?"

"I know your mother well."

"Does my dad know that?"

Porter blanched. "I don't know—I—I know *of* her. I follow her work. She's an incredible woman. And your brother, your eldest brother just walked away from the corporation. That was a shock move."

With a quick glance over his shoulder, Porter seemed to expect confirmation from Roxie. Except the woman was poring over the papers on the desk, lifting one to peek at another. Porter marched on over there to close the laptop and gather everything up.

"What?" Roxie asked, aiming for innocence. "It's not like I don't know what you're working on."

"Why did you bring me Tripp Breckenridge?"

"He's not *for* you. He's just here. He has a habit of it. Ignore him."

"Not easy to ignore a guy like him. Tripp Breckenridge, the most infamous of the Breckenridge Boys."

"Infamous?" Tripp asked. "Nah. I'm the handsomest Breckenridge, the most thoughtful, caring." Hmm, and would the world believe that? "Definitely the best lover." Though given the brothers didn't share women, there was no one qualified to verify that. "And you, sir, are Porter Clement. Got your heart broken by our own Roxanna Kyst here." Roxie's ex? "And are first chair on the Gambatto prosecution."

Shit—what? That line was for her. That's why they were in Chicago. This guy. Porter Clement.

"There's a squad of us," stated the modest prosecutor, "we're a team."

"I'll bet."

This wasn't a trip to see Trish or a second betrayer. Though Porter should be just as concerned about keeping his life as any turncoat. His place was torched... oh, God. Roxie brought her to the man gathering the facts. The man who had evidence maybe even Trish didn't have. Was it possible he knew more than Trish? The man was aware of strategy, the strength of the case, the chances of conviction. She hadn't even considered approaching the prosecution...

"Oh my God," she whispered, fixating on the man who'd been nothing to her a moment ago. "This is why we..." Her hand rose in his general direction while Roxie nodded. "He's the one prosecuting my brother, my family."

"Your—shit." Shock widened his mouth for a second. "You're Sequoia Gambatto." She forgave him a few moments of incredulity; her needle was stuck in the same groove. "You changed your hair."

That was why he hadn't recognized her? In his defense, Roxie and Tripp were the distracting types. He probably hadn't really looked.

"Since I was eighteen? Yes. I did. A few times."

"Eighteen. The last pictures of you were…" Porter said. "You went to college and never came back to Chicago."

She'd been back, though wouldn't admit that to this audience.

"My father and I had a falling out."

Among other things.

"You've been out of it for so long…" His demeanor changed. "Don't mistake me, I'm grateful, but how can you help us break down current operations?"

"Sequoia's not *for* you either." Roxie tsked. "Geez, what do you think I am? A matchmaker or a madam?"

"We only got Trish because of you."

"You only got Trish because of Zairn," Roxie said. "You remember how I reacted when I found out?"

Now she wanted to know how Roxie reacted. That wasn't exactly the best moment to ask.

"But you brought me her sister anyway."

"I didn't bring you her sister, I brought her sister to you. You're the gift, not the recipient."

Swiping something aside, Porter picked up a phone. "We can record this here or we can go to the office. It's late, but for something like this Tim will—"

"Whoa," Roxie said. "Grab those reins, big boy. It's not time to saddle up."

In an involuntary move, she took a step back and came up against Tripp who clasped her shoulders, holding her against him. She hadn't known he was there, yet he held her up. Tripp was one of those guys who didn't upset people. Unless he wanted to. He could be the most powerful force in the room or completely invisible.

She hadn't thought much about his presence, they'd known each other for... ever. Often he was part of the furniture in her life. Not right then. In that moment, she'd never been more grateful for him. Her surrogate brother would never let anyone hurt or harass her, which was ironic given that her biological brother, Joey, would happily sell her for scrap.

"I don't understand," Porter said, his hand with the phone sinking to the desk. "Sequoia, you don't want to testify? Why else would you come here? Why else would you want to talk to me? Are you here to plead for mercy?"

Quite the opposite. Did that make her a bad person? A selfish person? What kind of a person wanted to see their family behind bars? Wait, how many people did her father hurt and torment on a daily basis? Surely one outweighed the other. His guilt had to outweigh hers, whether he felt it or not.

"There is more to life than work, Porter, honey. And this is off the books."

"Off the books?"

"Completely," Tripp said. "As far as anyone else is concerned, this conversation never happened."

"I'm a public servant." Porter's edge of suspicion was understandable. "Anything shady—"

"Tripp looks the way he looks, we can't help the bad boy thing." Roxie tapped the desk. "The rest of us are squeaky clean... ish. All we need from you is some information. Just a few lousy words. That's not too much to ask given how much information we've funneled your way, wouldn't you say?"

He laughed. "You're just through telling me Zairn was my ticket. How does that mean I owe you something?"

"Him. Me. One and the same. You know I can

pull this any time."

The air got serious. "Don't play that card."

"What card?"

"You think I don't remember that night?" Porter asked. "Zairn got your permission. He needed your permission."

"It's not permission."

"You're threatening to have your boyfriend pull the deal. What happens to Trish then?"

"I'm not threatening anyone with anything." Roxie stood. "Let's have a drink. Take this kettle off the heat." Rounding the desk, Roxie paused to bounce up and kiss Porter's cheek. "I've missed you."

The former couple embraced. "Life's never the same without you around, RoRo."

FIFTEEN

AFTER A SQUEEZE of her shoulders, Tripp let go to go pour drinks.

"Catch up time!" Roxie announced. Sometimes she forgot how much there was to know about the new woman in her life. Ever the hostess, Roxie went to the living room and gestured at the seats. "Everyone sit down. Relax. Kick off your shoes." All eyes dropped to Roxie's bare feet. "I'm at home everywhere."

"Have you seen your father since you got back?" Porter asked, going to join Roxie, though it was Sequoia he wanted the answer from judging by the direction of his expectant gaze.

"My father—speaking of, why isn't he in jail?"

She wasn't surprised, but did doubt how slick this prosecutor could be if he let that slip by him.

"You really haven't kept up," Porter said. "He made bail."

Roxie sat at the end of the couch while Porter took a seat in an armchair. All very civilized.

"Why on earth would anyone let—"

"Probably best not to ask that question in Chicago," Roxie muttered from the corner of her mouth.

"Your father has influence," Tripp said from the kitchen.

Yeah, and bribed his way out. Plus he knew things, some things people might not want getting out. Damn, it was so unfair that he kept getting away with his bullshit.

Putting that aside, this was an opportunity to get answers. Except she didn't know this prosecutor guy, didn't know what he'd tell her or how much to trust him. Asking her sister was one thing, opening up to a stranger...

Okay, she was no slouch, how could she frame this? Hmm, ah, mental deep breath, and over she went to sit on the couch opposite Roxie.

"My brother didn't slip through the net."

"No offense, but your brother doesn't invite the same loyalty... or have the same smarts."

"And he doesn't have the best impulse control." Came from a lifetime of being spoiled and entitled. "It's better that he's there."

No doubt her father used some of his influence to keep Joey behind bars. Would he want a Gambatto back there? No, not exactly. Trouble with Joey was that he spent too much time getting in his own way.

"Now or in the long-term?" Porter asked.

And the prosecutor was invested in her potential answer, the discernment in his eye betrayed that. Porter was sizing her up. Just as she needed to get a measure of him, he clearly wanted a measure of her too. If he was to be honest, there would have to be trust. It wouldn't be easy for him to hand that out to a Gambatto, regardless of the history.

Could be that Tripp's showdown was coming in a different form than expected. But, seriously, who would she tell? At worst, it would be a Breckenridge and Porter already declared a proclivity for them. She definitely wouldn't be rushing back to her ancestral home to boast about gathering intelligence.

And what about him? This might be a casual conversation to her, was it to him? She didn't want to be called to the stand to relay any details of it further down the line.

"I have to be conscious—"

"Off the record," Porter said, relaxing into a smile that she wanted to trust.

His intuition was good. Did that make him better at his job? More likely to succeed? Another bias peeked through. Not bias, wishful thinking.

"It's strange being back in Chicago," she confessed, starting small. "Something in the air, just breathing it in…" Every little thing was a reminder of something, of the life she'd left behind. Like an ominous warning, if she stayed too long it might suck her back in. "I'm not usually so guarded in New York."

Or so serious and suspicious. Until then, she'd taken that freedom for granted. It was funny how fast a person could be transported back in time. Unsettling, actually. Would she always be a scared kid somewhere in her psyche?

"I assume you don't live the same lifestyle there."

As she had in Chicago as a child? As a teen? That was a lifetime ago, yet right there on her periphery all the time.

"In New York, I can trust the people around me…" for the most part. "But I'd be lying if I said my family don't still influence my decisions."

"We take care of each other in New York," Tripp said, approaching to distribute mixed drinks. She immediately put hers aside on the end table. "Seq's not so good at remembering that."

"Given her upbringing, I can forgive her."

Back then, forgetting could mean injury or worse. Where she'd been was one thing; where she'd end up mattered more. Don't languish, progress. The past wouldn't change, the road ahead was still to be built.

"Are you pursuing a case against my father?" In truth, she couldn't remember a time when there hadn't been some agency or department building a file on him. "Realistically. A case that might actually end somewhere around twenty-five to life."

All the years of investigation, paperwork, surveillance, files got thicker until he probably had his own row in the file room. Yet not one charge stuck. He was Teflon, that's what he told people as he laughed at feeble attempts by law enforcement to trap him behind bars. His arrogance was sickening, but it was difficult not to believe him invincible when he rose over and over again.

"There are a number of charges leveled at him," Porter said. "We're taking as many of his men from the streets as we can."

No one would cut a deal, if that was the expectation. Fewer soldiers on the streets explained the Gambattos shrinking territory. There was no one around to stake a claim, to defend what they asserted was theirs. The reduced manpower made it difficult to hold onto any respectable amount of control. And by respectable, she meant to the other families, the families who'd poached most of the Gambatto territory. The Gambattos were weak and there was no mercy in this town. The other families could have at it, for all she cared, she wouldn't be raising her children there... If she had children.

"What are the odds, Mr. Clement? Is there a chance he'll be taken off the street for good?"

"The more evidence we have, the better."

Her eyes met Tripp's as he sat beside her. "Time to call Axon?" he asked.

Another of the Breckenridge brothers. One of two security specialists in the family.

"No," she said, her head shaking.

Except Tripp could see through her façade into the workings of her mind. Maybe that was the key to the whole thing. Witness protection—private or federal. Her father wouldn't be able to reach her if she was in hiding. And Breck? She'd tell him to stay behind in New York with the people who loved him, but what would be the point? He wouldn't listen to that request any more than she would in his shoes.

And, truth be told, the only reason to get into the witness box would be to put her father away. Someone may ask why she'd testify. The answer was to free them, to be with Breck, that was why. She'd put her father in a cage to liberate her relationship. There was that selfish bone again; her Gambatto blood had to be curtailed.

Her head was in the clouds. What would be the point of freeing them only to disappear into hiding? She wouldn't. That meant if she testified and disappeared, Breck would be right there with her.

But the thing with Breck? They were polar opposites in family and upbringing. His family, their stability, meant everything to him. Would she steal him away from that?

"I would never do that to your mother," she said to Tripp as though he'd been reading her mind. "To your family."

"We can protect the Breckenridges if—"

"The Breckenridges don't need your protection," Tripp said to Porter. "She's talking about taking my brother with her because we both know he'll never watch her walk away alone."

"I can talk to him if—"

"It doesn't matter," she interjected. "Like you said, I've been gone too long. I don't know anything about current Gambatto operations."

"We're open to historical allegations. Anything you can give us to point—"

"This isn't what I wanted," she said. "I'm not here to testify against my father or to get myself in deeper." She hadn't known she was coming "here" at all, not to the prosecutor's residence. Getting sucked back and could happen fast. Not only suspicious, she had to be wary too. "I want my father in prison; he's a danger to society and that's where he belongs." True. And it sure sounded good, better than the lustful truth. "But this started as a case against my brother, Joey. Is that where it ends? Is he who you want?"

If they stopped there, ultimately, nothing would change, not for her.

"Joey's conviction is almost guaranteed," Porter said. "With what Trish knows, he'll be convicted of Ava Marilyn's murder."

Miss Illinois. God, it was sickening. How could anyone think they had the right to take another life? That woman had been in her prime and Joey cut her down. Why? She didn't know. Any reason would be a pitiful excuse.

"Will you make a deal?" she asked, knowing that was one way to achieve his ends.

"The case is strong enough that we don't have to. Though there's a chance of Joey working something out in California. They're desperate to get at him."

Was it a surprise her brother was wanted in more than one state? No. Though she didn't know the particulars.

"California?"

"Dayah Lynn," Roxie said. "He's going down for Dayah's murder too?"

The look Roxie and Porter exchanged was curious.

"Dayah Lynn," she murmured, her fingers linking with Tripp's. "The actress? Joey murdered her?"

The beauty's death made headlines at the time, a couple of years ago, at least.

"According to Trish," Roxie said.

Why did it feel like something wasn't being said. "What does that mean?"

Porter sighed. "LA could never make murder."

"Until Trish put the pieces together."

The true pieces or... otherwise?

"The whole case rests on Trish's word, from what I can tell. We don't know what happened," Porter said. "LA is working with Trish as much as they can to piece it all together. I don't know the specifics of their case and access is difficult."

"But California is not interested in convicting my father of anything?"

Porter's brow creased. "For the most part, the Gambattos are a Chicago problem. They have satellite divisions throughout—"

"I know that. I know there are tentacles all over. I also know without my father at the helm, those tentacles can be better pursued and eliminated."

"California's DA, Ackley, is heading the investigation into what happened to Dayah."

"And he declared her death murder at the time," Roxie said. "He's hungry to prove himself right."

"It's high profile," Porter stated, "and Ackley's taken a great personal interest in the case."

Roxie scoffed. "Too personal."

After Dayah's death, it hadn't taken long for the nubile beauty's love interest, Zairn Lomond, to land in DA Ackley's crosshairs. Yep, that Zairn. Horrifying. It was absolutely horrifying that anyone could even think...

Obviously, in the long run, it was proved Zairn had nothing to do with the young starlet's death. Still, damage had been done; Roxie's derision was understandable. If anyone tried to pin anything like that on Breck, she'd never forgive them, cleared or not.

"Going by Trish's testimony, Joey killed Dayah, though he's not admitting to it," Porter continued. "Ackley's not letting it go; I wouldn't be surprised if he tries to go around Joey to get to your father. Even if he can't pin anything on him, the scrutiny wouldn't be appreciated by your kin. Pissing them off increases the likelihood of Ackley getting a deal with Joey. But, honestly, you'd have to ask Ackley."

"You think he'll talk to us?" Roxie asked. "Why won't he talk to you? I thought you two were bestest buddies."

"Bestest buds because he called me about Zairn's connection to Ava a year ago?" Porter exhaled. "I thought we were over that. Until this case, I barely got our SA to talk to me. What's the odds on me being on the inside of a case two thousand miles away? Zairn must know someone over there."

Her hand tightened in Tripp's. If Zairn didn't, Tripp would. Ackley was near the top of the chain. Would anyone in the Golden State risk pissing him off?

"Ackley is a stubborn, arrogant—he cares about nothing except himself."

"Think you're biased, RoRo?" Porter asked Roxie. "He did try to finger your fiancé."

At that time, Roxie and Zairn didn't know each other existed. Didn't matter, some wounds never fully healed.

"Biased or not, the only way to get answers would be to rock up and get in front of him."

"We can do that," Tripp said. "Whatever we need to do. We do have a jet after all."

"Our State's Attorney, Tim Unst, has the reins on the web of your father's case. If you talk to him, you'll get a better picture of how it might play out, but he'll tell you the same as I will: there's no guarantee."

Especially when there was a chance of money or power changing hands.

"Give me it straight," she said, shifting to the edge of her seat. "The Gambattos are losing territory, that means they're losing money. If my father walks away from this, if you don't get a conviction, will he take back what he's lost?"

Was there any hope he might be out of the game for good?

Before responding, Porter took a deep breath. "If you asked any of the other families, they'd tell you the Gambattos are done." Bravado? "We've been going hard and the feds aren't far behind." So if the city failed to secure a conviction, the country may step up. "But I, personally, wouldn't put money on anything either way. I've seen stranger things happen."

Great, just the answer she didn't want.

"If Gambatto Senior is convicted, do the chances of recovery go down?" Well meaning, Tripp supported her, but she couldn't rely on her father going to prison if even the prosecutor wasn't sure it would happen. "Can he run things from the inside?"

"It's not like it used to be. No more steak dinners and hot baths every night. That said, in prison, he's likely to live better than any other inmate."

"I don't care about his life in there," she said, blood hot. "I care about what he can do to those on the outside."

To her. To Breck.

"I can't answer that with any certainty." Just what did this guy know? "What I will say is, although there's no guarantee he'll be convicted, there's also no guarantee of anything being left at the end. This will drag on for years. We'll take Joey down, then California will. At some point your father will face his reckoning. Make no mistake, it will be damaging."

Damaging enough?

"You can't live your life under threat of the what-ifs," Roxie said, shifting to reach over Tripp and take her hand. "The best-case scenario is as likely to happen as the worst case."

"Moreso," Porter said. "Assuming you want your father in prison or ruined. The other families won't let him just stroll in and take over again. The McDades are strengthening their power base every day."

Which could indicate the Irish would be more inclined to murder her father than put up with any attempt at poaching bullshit.

If it was just her, she'd live with that. But Breck was in New York dismantling his life to show her that even if her father wanted something from them, they wouldn't be able to provide it. What if he did all that and her father did go to prison and lose his authority?

He'd be nothing. It wasn't so hard to laugh in the face of nothing.

A phone rang. Tripp's. They sat so close that it buzzed against her thigh.

Raising his hips, he retrieved it and then his jaw moved.

"What?" she asked, recognizing his hesitation. Though asking the question was sort of dumb. "It's Breck, isn't it?" He half shrugged, his thumb moving toward the—"I'll answer it." She presented her palm, he didn't seem sure. "You want to lie to him?"

SIXTEEN

TRIPP PUT THE PHONE in her hand; she answered while getting to her feet.

"Hey, stranger," she said, stepping around Tripp's legs to stride over the living room.

"Take a hit in a sensitive spot? Voice is higher than it used to be, brother."

On a smile, she opened the front door to go into the hallway. It may not be complete privacy, but she'd prefer to keep as much sense as possible.

"Am I not good enough? Did you need your beloved brother for something specific?"

"Yeah," Breck said. "Tracking down my roommate."

Right. Roommate.

And if anyone needed to know something, Tripp was the guy to call. Maybe bringing him wasn't the smartest move.

Best to go with a tease. "We ran away together."

"Uh huh. You tell me it's not a problem to stay here, then disappear."

So he was at her place? Good. Hopefully he'd

think straighter there... but not too straight.

"I didn't disappear, don't be dramatic," she droned. "Something came up. I have to... handle it. That's all. No big deal."

"And you called my brother? Is it illegal?"

She scoffed, keeping the tease going. "Why would you ask that?"

"That's the only reason you'd call Tripp instead of me."

"You'd do illegal things for me..." Resting against the wall, she flattened one hand between it and her coccyx and lowered her chin. "Wouldn't you, baby?"

"Hard to be an active parent to our child if I'm in prison."

"There's no baby, I told you that. And maybe I called Tripp because he still has access to his trust fund. He didn't take crazy pills like someone else I know."

"If you needed money, you'd call my dad, and I didn't cancel your credit card."

No, because he'd never do something like that. Whoa but wait, who exactly would be making payments if the guy on the hook for it didn't have a job?

"It's not about money. Tripp's just here. He has a habit of it."

Thank you, Roxie. The woman wasn't wrong.

"Tell me where you are and I'll have a habit of it too."

"You're good on the phone. I love how you tease me."

Though it was conversations like this that made living together a risky proposition. Thank God she'd left the state. If they started having sex again...

"Think you can flirt me into submission?"

"It's worked before."

"Your phone's going straight to voicemail, which means you turned it off." Specifically so he couldn't track her. He'd noticed that, huh? "Doesn't support your theory. You're avoiding me, which means you don't trust yourself to lie to me."

"I'm not lying, and my phone is elsewhere right now." It was in her purse in the apartment above… and, yes, off, a minor, irrelevant detail. "But you found me. No harm done."

"There's harm done if you're keeping something from me." Now there was an accusation. "The money matter that much to you?"

When her mouth opened, a squeak of offense followed. "I'm going to pretend that was a bad joke." He needled her to provoke a reaction and she fell for it every time. "How dare you say that to me, Stat." The guy was under pressure and he was right, she was withholding. Except she couldn't fill him in, not yet. Time to flip the mood. "Now if you'd asked me if the sex mattered that much…"

"Come home and you can have it."

Home. Her guy. Her apartment. The proposition was tempting. Her yearning come to life.

"This is my issue, and we shouldn't do this." When would she learn the flirting always led them down the same path? "You shouldn't give up on everything—"

"You won't change my mind."

She sighed. "I know." If anyone would be able to, it would be her. Even she knew better when his mind was made up. "You have your reasons for doing what you're doing. Can't you trust I have my reasons too?"

"I feel better knowing Tripp's with you. You at Crimson?"

"I plead the fifth."

"Because you don't want me to come over there or because you're not?"

Her lips curled before she laughed. "You missed

your calling. Ever think about the law?"

"Can't afford college."

And he was doing it again. "I have a good job, I can support you through it."

"Baby comes first."

"You think law school will be easier with an infant to care for?"

"You asked first, it's only fair."

"Maybe you could stay home with him full-time. Momma brings the bacon and daddy keeps the home."

"Coy, I'd do it in a heartbeat."

"That's because you'd do anything for me."

He'd been raised with more traditional gender roles, sure, but that wouldn't stop him living the life that suited them. Given his reputation, many people would struggle to visualize him with a baby in his arms. She couldn't think of anything sexier. Breck was the most caring, patient human being she'd ever known.

"Come home."

And the one thing he was asking, she was refusing. Not permanently, just for now.

"Stop saying that." Closing her eyes, she fought her natural instinct to give in to him. "You call it home and give me hope, it's not fair."

"There's more than hope. I'm here, baby. I'll fix this. Whatever it takes."

"You know this was never what I wanted, right? That I never expected you to give up your birthright, your family, your purpose."

"You are my family and my purpose, Coy. If I haven't shown you that by now—"

"This is an us problem; it's not on you to fix it. I might not agree with the way you're pursuing the ends, but I'm trying to do the same."

"Find a way for us to be together."

"It shouldn't be this difficult. Don't you wonder

if fate is trying to tell us something?"

"I don't believe in that. We make our own fate, there's no destiny desperate to pull us apart. Haven't I taught you that a challenge is simply an opportunity to flex your muscles? The harder a victory's won, the more it's appreciated. Just ask my mom."

Ah, the story of his parents' beginning. "Yes, I'd have to ask your mom, because if I asked your dad, he'd say Alice created barriers that didn't exist."

"Huh, interesting way to put it. Maybe if she'd just trusted him…"

Her throat quivered because he was thinking the same thing about her. Except it wasn't about erecting barriers, not between them, those barriers went around him. It was her duty to protect the man she loved.

Except that was just it, she loved him. They loved each other, and she wasn't the only one who deserved a little hope.

"There's no future without you," she said. "It's just… blank."

"Agreed. So we have no choice, we're going to do this. We fucked around with it for years and I have to admit…"

"Admit?" she prompted because it wasn't like him to censor himself, especially with her.

They could say anything to each other. Anything. Was that true? Why wasn't she telling him the truth of her location and what she was doing? Because he'd want to be with her, and she couldn't let this toxicity touch him. And they'd only forget they weren't supposed to…

"Some part of me always assumed you'd get over it."

"Get over my family poisoning yours?" She could believe he believed that, which proved he didn't understand the depth of her fear. "There's nothing I wouldn't do for your family or their integrity. Just being together… Have you never considered what people thought when they saw us together?"

"You know I don't care about the opinion of others."

No, he might not, that didn't mean those opinions didn't do damage.

"They saw us together, and everyone in New York knows you." In the Breckenridge circles anyway. "They didn't know me, and whenever someone asked, you want to know what they said to identify me?"

"You're the smartest, most beautiful woman in the country?"

The flatness of his words proved he anticipated where she was going.

"They said I was a Gambatto. That my heritage contradicts yours. They look at us and judge both of us for tainting the pure, wholesome Breckenridge brand."

"And if you thought I gave a damn about the brand—"

"Think about more than yourself," she beseeched. "The work your parents do—"

"My mom adores you, and don't even get me started on how much my father values you. It would hurt if they found out this was why you kept us apart. You're worrying about New York society—"

"It's more than New York society."

"And we're not living in the fucking Victorian era. I love who I love and I won't apologize for that."

"Our children would be at risk. If my father learned we had a child, he would've been a threat to them the moment I said he wasn't allowed near them."

"Two of my brothers specialize in security. Our child would never be at risk."

She sighed. "You've made your choice. Let me make mine."

"You are my choice."

One of them would have to surrender. "I love you."

"And that's enough." His voice softened. "That's it. All we need. Come home, Coy, and we'll figure this out together."

"I will," she whispered. "I will come home. Just not yet."

"Because…?"

"These are my demons. If I'm going to get over this, I have to do this my way. Trust me, Stat, please."

He exhaled. Yes, there was irritation there, but there was resignation too. "You have until you're next ovulating." She smiled. "We have a job to do."

"The only one you have right now. Breck Breckenridge unemployed, who'd have thought it?"

"Actually, I've been inundated with offers." No surprise there. "Nothing suitable yet."

"Because every Fortune 500 is clamoring for you. And you can't have a job that pays well? Are you really the only person on the planet coveting poverty?"

"There's no poverty if we're together, Coy. Our child will want for nothing. Breckenridges have more than money in abundance."

"Love."

"Yes."

"Support not judgment."

"I see you've met us before."

"It doesn't matter how low your wage is, if my father is still playing his games, he'll expect you to make demands on your family. I won't allow them, or the Breckenridge name, to be exploited like that. I appreciate what you're doing, but you'll always have access to their means. Their money and their name."

"A name can be changed."

God, it tore at her. The Breckenridges had pride in themselves, not in conceit, but in their integrity. It sickened her that he thought he'd have to renounce that dignity to be with her. She'd move to Mars before letting that happen.

"Your children will have the Breckenridge name," she said, "whether they're mine or not."

He'd demanded she promise no other man would father her children. She'd never make the same demand in return. He deserved love and optimism. The more time passed, the more she feared Alice's prediction would come true.

Sucking her lips around her teeth, this was the crux of the issue. He'd never give up on her, on them, so there was only one thing for it. She had to do whatever was necessary to take down the Gambattos.

Betray her own blood for the man she loved? Yes, no hesitation. Why hadn't she done it years ago?

SEVENTEEN

HER FATHER WOULDN'T trust her. That wasn't offensive, she wouldn't trust him either and didn't believe in double standards. Rocking up to his doorstep would more likely seal her in his prison than free her to be with Breck. And appealing to his better nature? Ha! What better nature? If that was even a remote possibility, she'd have done it years ago.

After hanging up on Breck last night, she'd popped back into Porter's apartment to tell the others she was going to bed. Her decision needed some time to percolate.

The Gambattos could not regain power. Her father couldn't. She'd lived her whole life believing he got whatever he wanted, that he was the most important figure on the planet. It was hard to cast off that image when it had been ingrained in her since birth.

But this was a new day, time for a new outlook.

His arrogance would be his downfall. Even now, privately or not, she'd bet he believed this whole investigation was nothing more than an inconvenience.

He'd have faith in triumph, his own anyway. Joey would lose his freedom. Their father would accept that as the price of doing business. In his own warped mind, Joey deserved to be locked up for being careless, Senior was too important to be taken down.

Joey did deserve prison, but her father did too.

She got up early. Okay, that was a slight lie. Sleep hadn't come easy. Rather than battle insomnia, she left her bed to go to Roxie's desk, swiping a few sheets of paper from the printer. A few became a few more; the pen worked on its own, getting as much down as possible. By the time she was done, her hand cramped and light peeked through the curtains.

New dawn.

No one else was awake. Not that she considered that before leaving Roxie's to hurry downstairs. Knocking on Porter's front door, she wanted to get in and out before anyone noticed her absence. What time was it? She hadn't thought to check. Oops.

Adrenaline raced her heart. This was a bad idea on so many levels. It went against the cells that made up her being. It was almost as if basic genetics imprinted an aversion to turning on her family. Out of guilt? Or was it fear?

She knocked again. What was taking so long? Could it be so early Porter wasn't up yet? Alternatively, it was later and he'd already gone to work. Please don't say it was the latter. The last thing she wanted to do was walk up to the prosecutor's office where anyone could see her. The idea was to gain her freedom, not incite her enemies into acting against her and those she loved.

Another knock. Maybe slightly more insistent than the last. Rudeness had its place in urgency. It wasn't bad manners, more like determination. Yes, determination was a good word. Boy, could she convince herself of anything.

She'd apologize later. Send Porter some expensive scotch or fancy cufflinks, whatever Roxie said he liked. Being friends with the ex wasn't a bad deal while attempting to keep someone on her side.

There was reason behind the madness; it wasn't just random insanity. No, she saved that for Breck. This mission had to be completed while she had the gumption to do it. Translated: before she talked herself out of it. If it took a whole day—God knew how long Porter stayed at work. Guys like him didn't stick to a typical nine-to-five. Something she had experience with.

But it was the weekend. Would he go into work at the weekend? This was a big case, probably a seven day a week deal. If not, sleeping in may be more—

A click prompted her back a small step. Yes! There was someone on the—hair wet, Porter was tying a robe when he opened the door.

"Knew it couldn't be Rox, she'd never be up this early on a Saturday."

Days of the week versus weekends probably didn't factor much into Roxie's decision making these days. Her life was the same and different every day of the week. Irrelevant. Get to the point. The man hadn't been disturbed for no reason. From the look of him, he'd been in the shower. Impressive that he'd heard the door at all.

Despite vigilant building security, the danger posed by her relatives probably hung heavy on him. Maybe he was conscious of every little noise. Paranoid? No. Smart. As she was all too aware. She glanced around the doorframe feeling a tickle of it herself. Could be there were cameras somewhere she didn't see.

Shit. The point. Right.

"I have something for you," she said, holding her stack of papers aloft. "Something…"

"That might help the prosecution?"

Quick study. "No one can know. Not even

Roxie."

"It's about your family."

Obviously, what else would be of interest to him? What else did they have in common? A love of Alice Breckenridge, but that wasn't a truth she'd keep hidden.

"Can you keep it between us?" The guy could lie, but she had to hear the words anyway. "If this sits uncomfortably for you—"

"Come in," he said, stepping aside to let her enter.

Despite being there the previous night, she waited, as was polite, until he led her over to the desk and gestured for her to sit.

She settled herself. "You didn't give me an answer."

"Can I keep it between us? Depends what it is," he said, pulling his chair around to sit at the end of the desk. Less confrontational, more conversational. The guy was good. "I won't make any false promises. Roxie doesn't know every detail about my life. My boss on the other hand, if it helps the case—"

"It can't get out that I was the one to provide this. I won't testify. I won't sign any affidavits or put my name on anything. As far as the world is concerned, this never happened."

"If you have evidence of criminality, I need to be able to use it. That means chain of custody. Without that, whatever you share may be useless. Zairn is protecting your sister, she trusted him to—"

"No," she said, adamant. "I'm not doing this for me. I'm not even doing it because it's the right thing to do." A shameful thing to admit. "I'm doing this to be with the man that I love." With that clarity, Porter's shoulders went back as he sagged a little. Did he judge her? He should; she judged herself. "I can't be with him if I'm always looking over my shoulder."

His nod was slow yet understanding. "What have you got for me?"

Still no definitive answer on secrecy. Nothing was set in stone yet, she could still get up and walk out. Except that would be tantamount to walking out on Breck. Damnit.

"Why did you and Roxie break up?"

The question just popped out. Yeah, okay, maybe it wasn't her business, but if she was going to entrust her future to this guy, his honesty was important too. If he was cagey with her, why should she be open with him? She'd confessed the truth about her motivation, that was personal. Didn't that give her the right to ask a personal question in return?

"I proposed," he said with a flash of a smile. "That was enough to scare her off."

She winced. "And then she went and got engaged to Zairn?"

He shrugged. "Z worked hard for it and Rox didn't want to be a congressman's wife…" Oh, wow, a man of ambition. "It's a long story. I'm happy for them. Roxie's a dynamic woman, she needs the life Zairn gives her." The excitement? The unpredictability? "They're a better match than Rox and I were. I didn't see it at the time, I see it now. No hard feelings."

What happens when the person you see in your forever walks away? Something she didn't want her or Breck to learn.

"Magnanimous of you."

"Zairn's a good guy. I wanted to hate him," he said, raising his hands. "Everything I thought I knew about his reputation, and he was moving in on my ex…"

"Moving in or moved in?"

"Then the guy went and lined up a star witness." Hmm, the prosecutor was good at ducking questions. "How could I hate him after that?"

"One step closer to congressman."

An exhaled laugh. "Yeah, I guess so."

"You must still be close if you're living in their building."

"These days I talk more to Zairn than to Rox. He kind of keeps a lid on things for her. She needs him in a way she never needed me. Not in a dependent type way, they complement each other. He takes care of the details, she focuses on bullshit he'd rather not deal with. She's amazing for the brand, plays to it, I think."

"I've got to say she fits in with his set so well, sometimes better than him. It's a relief for him to just sit back and watch her work. No one works a room as well as her." Or so she'd heard. "She's a natural."

"Cares though, more than people think. The frivolous thing works sometimes, but if she needs to switch it on, she can. I remember the night she heard about the fire at my apartment. Man, was she pissed I'd taken on the Gambatto case. And this was after we were broken up. Even still, she called as soon as she heard, read me the riot act. Would've done anything to get me to give it up."

After they were broken up. Huh. That was something. In college, there had been guys, boyfriends, but her relationship with Breck was unique. She'd never cared for another man the way she did for him. From that aspect, she had no frame of reference. Love for Breck was automatic and the care came by default. If she found out he was putting himself in danger, she'd go nuts too. Casual college hookups, the men before him, didn't inspire that same fervor.

If Porter proposed to Roxie, the relationship must've been serious. Feelings didn't go away overnight. No matter how acrimonious or amicable the split, Roxie hadn't hesitated to call Porter and let him know she was worried. No, more than that, the riot act suggested anger, panic. The man had once been the most important in her life, and Roxie hadn't switched that off. Maybe their love took on a different hue, but it was still love.

Was that enough? Had Porter shown enough trust to gain hers? If she didn't want Roxie or Tripp to know about this meeting, she didn't have a lot of time to sit and shoot the shit.

Big breath. "My father has five safe deposit boxes."

The physical paper didn't have to be handed over yet. Baby steps.

Porter stiffened just a little, adopting a stance that betrayed his transfer to work mode. "In the city?"

"Not all of them." In both hands, she held the sheets a little closer to her chest. "I have a file in New York, if I'd known we were coming here..."

Would she have brought it? Probably not. She barely looked at the heavy weight it represented. Roxie did the right thing keeping their destination secret. If she'd known Chicago was their goal, she wouldn't have got on the plane. Now she was there, it might work out for the best. Emphasis on the *might*. In her family, the unpredictable flared whenever it felt like it.

"We can arrange to pick up—"

"No," she said, shaking her head and putting the papers on the desk. Not for him, not yet. "I've written down as much as I can remember. When I'm back in New York, if there's anything I've missed..."

"Did you take it from him? The file? Does it belong to your father?"

"No." She swallowed. "It's mine." And her burden to bear alone, until now anyway. "As a teenager, when I learned more about what my father did and how dangerous he was, our relationship..."

"Soured?"

Good word. "Yes. I didn't want to be a

Gambatto if it meant hurting people." And worse. "The way he treated people… There were different versions of him, sometimes I didn't see the same one twice in a day. There was no reasoning with him, no understanding, no compassion. I didn't want to live my life that way. Being a Gambatto, all that came with it…" This was irrelevant. She was rambling. "Anyway, I started collecting what I could, little things, taking notes, no gotcha moments exactly, but there are things I know, things that might help."

"Because if he's in prison, he can't influence your relationship with the man you mentioned."

Influence. Something her father craved. Much as she didn't want to admit it, some part of her had to concede his influence wouldn't leave her completely, even if he was encased in concrete walls. As for her and Breck? She'd always kept her father as far from her personal life as possible, but wasn't naïve enough to think he didn't keep tabs on her when it suited him.

After all this time, he wouldn't expect her to turn against him. No, that wasn't right, he'd known they were against each other since her teen years. But to actively do something that would hurt him? He'd doubt she had the ability. Maybe she didn't. Maybe nothing she'd collected would mean anything or help the prosecution. Still, she had to try.

"I want freedom to have a future. One that doesn't end in prison or hiding. You know, Joey's an asshole who deserves to be punished, but he's also who he is because of my father. Yes, he's taken it too far and can never be forgiven, but our father wormed his way into our psyche's young."

Like brainwashing or grooming. Once upon a time, she'd worshipped her father, looked up at him with adoring eyes, beholding him as the best of humanity. Naïveté reigned when she played with dolls and tea sets.

It was whittled down piece by piece until the moment it struck her that he was the worst of men. Despite his actions being the cause, she carried so much shame for the association. Like blood stained her skin, she could scrub and scrub, but it would always come right back.

"Trish is immune," Porter said.

That was supposed to be optimistic, to make her feel better? Too bad she disagreed.

"No—" Except it wasn't her place. "I suppose I shouldn't speak in absolutes, it's been a long time since we talked. Maybe you're right. Could be she's had a whole personality transplant."

And who knew what Trish had endured that immunized her to their father's hegemony.

"I wouldn't say that. She's vibrant. He hasn't broken her, this hasn't broken her."

"How often do you see her?"

An exhaled laugh joined the whisper of a smile. "I don't know if I should answer that. I have to be conscious of her safety."

Good. Yes, the implication she'd hurt her sister was offensive, but she couldn't be a hypocrite. Hadn't she wondered if Porter took Trish's wellbeing seriously? He was gaining points, sure, but she'd love Breck's take. He wasn't there. And whose fault was that?

Breck was an amazing judge of character. No, he didn't have a lot of patience for people who wasted his time or tried to take liberties. He sized people up quick, picked up on signals she sometimes missed. Roxie might be a new friend, but Alice liked her. So if Roxie trusted Porter enough to be in a relationship with him, should she trust in that?

"My sister was always harder than me, better at the intimidation stuff." For a time, Trish embraced that life. Something must've changed. And it was on her that she wasn't around to be a part of that development. "She deserves your loyalty. Thank you for looking after her."

"That's all on Zairn. He does most of the handholding too. For what it's worth, I'm impressed by her strength and have never doubted her sincerity. She's been through a lot."

Alone. That's what she heard. Trish had been through a lot alone, without a sister at her side. Any time she thought of contacting her sister, she'd talked herself out of it, deciding all she could do was be receptive if Trish reached out. She didn't want to put her sister in the awkward position of go-between after all. God, what a lousy excuse.

"We were so different. She looked out for me, protected me from a lot of it. I suppose I saw strength, her impervious nature, her ability to deflect and avoid. It never seemed like she needed me."

"You should talk to Zairn. I think he'd have a lot to tell you. The kind of things neither of them would tell me."

She should go to Zairn, to apologize for ducking what should've been partly her responsibility too. With her sister out of the game, separated from the family, there was no reason they shouldn't reconnect. If Trish wanted to reconnect. She didn't want to endanger her either, or be seen as an access point. That wouldn't leave her and Breck much safer. And what about Trish? Could be once this was all over, she wanted to be left alone to build her new life.

After another slow, deep breath, she laid her palm on the papers.

"I'll take you through this, as much as I can. Some of the details, dates and times, etc. I'll get those to you later." Though she'd have to ensure it was done without leaving a trail. Trust only went so far with a man who may have to prove provenance. "What's in here will give you leads to follow. New avenues to explore.

Anything you find from this anonymous tip…"
Widening her eyes, she waited for his single nod of
understanding. "Could help you, or the feds, with the
prosecution. Now I am not a source, you can't call me
up and ask questions, this is it. A one-shot deal. Take it
or leave it."

He shifted to the edge of the chair, getting closer
to the tantalizing stack that saw him almost salivate.

"I'll take it," he said. "Let's get started."

EIGHTEEN

WITHOUT KNOWING HER arrival time, she couldn't tell how long her and Porter had been talking in his apartment. However long it was, the guy had time to get dressed and make coffee. For a while now, he'd been pacing, scrutinizing one handwritten page he'd taken from the others.

"This is incredible."

"It happened a long time ago," she said.

"There's no statute of limitation on murder."

No, she knew that. "I mean not all of the players are still involved." And it would be flat cruel to draw them back in. "We don't even know if they're still alive."

"But you think she's still alive?" he asked, raising the pulp. "This Rosita?"

"The last time I saw her, she was alive. But we're talking years since then, I can't say that now."

"Your father cared for her."

"If he didn't, she wouldn't have been allowed to live long enough for me to see her again."

"You can testify in court. Tell the—"

"No, I told you no. I was a teenager and it was a million years ago. Besides, isn't whatever she told me hearsay? I didn't see it happen myself."

"But you did see their intimacy. You witnessed their affair."

More times than she cared to admit. "My father always had mistresses. Sometimes they lasted the night, sometimes it was years."

"Have you written them down?" he asked, marching back to the desk. "Their names, the dates you—"

"I didn't always know their names or the dates they slept with my father."

Which was a ridiculous enough thing to say that he should appreciate the absurdity of the question. Those women, the ones who'd broken free, it wouldn't be fair to drag them back. They'd have new lives now, and maybe the people in them wouldn't want to know about their pasts.

"If we know their names, details, we can trace them, find out what they know."

"They could be anywhere by now."

"We have people who do this kind of thing full-time. And the more names we have, the better. If nothing else, it adds to the timeline, gives more context. You never know what detail could be crucial."

"Involving them puts them at risk. It's not safe. You should know that as well as anyone; someone connected to my family will be responsible for flambeeing your apartment. Think about that. How many other people will get hurt if you start harassing them?"

Which was exactly the reason she hadn't put identifying information down for those she considered just passing through. Fleeting connections didn't tend to lead to the sharing of incriminating information. But what did that matter? If anyone loyal to the Gambattos saw investigators and law enforcement sneaking around with someone, they wouldn't stop to give that someone the benefit of the doubt. Shoot first, ask questions later. What was another life? Innocent or not.

"How much harm will your father do over the next five years, ten years, if we can't put him in jail?"

Damnit, yeah, okay, there was that. Didn't Porter get that she didn't have to be convinced? How many more lives would…?

"You have to promise me you'll be careful, discreet, and the information didn't come from me. I don't want them in the witness box, not unless you can promise to protect them." Could anyone official do that a hundred percent? "No coercion. And their details didn't come from me. Do not mention my name to them, to anyone."

"Absolutely. Whatever you need."

On a sigh, she opened her hand. "Do you have a pen?"

This was a bad idea, she was getting drawn back in herself. See how easily it could happen? It snuck up on her. This was why she didn't come back to Chicago. God, and what was worse? All she kept thinking was how much she wanted Breck there. She could be impulsive, maybe didn't think everything through. And what happened in those situations? Breck caught her hand, pulled her back and just looked into her eyes until she got it. They didn't need words to communicate, but she did need contact. Physical contact.

One phone call and—no, there was a reason she'd turned her phone off. She should've left it in New York, that would've been the smarter plan.

Almost done with her list, a sound from upstairs stopped the pen on the paper. Was that a door slamming? Footsteps, fast, slow, a pause…

"Who's that?" she asked. "Someone's upstairs."

"People come and go around here," Porter said. "Could be anyone."

"Is it Roxie?"

"That sounded more like the front door," he said. "Could be Rainie, Trevor, Zairn, I don't—"

"Zairn? Why would he—"

"Roxie's here," he said with a shrug. "I think. God knows with that woman. Disappearing at two a.m. would be exactly her style, especially recently."

Being ditched was preferrable over Zairn showing up unannounced. How would she hold up under his scrutiny? And Roxie wouldn't lie to him if asked straight out why they were there, would she? She shouldn't be promoting conflict in others' relationships, and what else did secrets cause?

The movement noises continued, then the mumble of a muffled voice. Now there was more than one person up there. Great.

On edge, she put the pen down. "Shit, I thought I could get back before they knew I was gone."

"We still have work to do."

"No," she said and stood up. "I don't want anyone to come looking for me. What am I supposed to tell Roxie?"

"Tell her you went for a walk."

Oh, yeah, brilliant. "Alone on Chicago streets where anyone could recognize me?" And this guy was supposed to be smart. "You think she'll buy that?"

"No," Porter said. "But she'll let you get away with it. She'll believe when you're ready, you'll tell her. Otherwise, your business is your business. She won't push."

Nice to know, though the same may not be said for Tripp. He wouldn't push, but he might ask, repeatedly. At least she could be sure neither would tell

Breck about her momentary disappearance. Tripp because he never told anyone's secrets to others, and Roxie because, well, she didn't know Breck all that much. Why would they ever have cause to seek each other out or talk...? Although... wasn't he going to the wedding? Shit. Was anyone not going to the wedding of the century? Roxie could tell Alice... hmm... No, she wouldn't... would she?

Alice was lethal when it came to secrets. Her kindness, the soft note of her voice, probing without being invasive. That woman could give CIA interrogators a run for their money with nothing more than a smile.

The longer she loitered in Porter's apartment, the harder walking into Roxie's would be.

"Okay, I'm going upstairs."

"What about the names?" he asked, leaping into her way on route to the door.

"I'll finish later, you've got enough to go on." Now he was just being rude. "I'll put a note under your door later. Are you going into work?"

"Planned to. I can wait. I'll come upstairs—"

"No, you won't," she said, planting a hand on his chest when he tried to go around her. "Roxie won't buy the walk story if we're together. What kind of walk includes her ex-boyfriend?"

"She won't be jealous."

A tsk. "I don't care about jealous." It wouldn't be nice to laugh in his face. If he thought anyone would ever put them together in an intimate way... Wasn't his fault he'd never seen her and Breck in action. "I care about answering questions that might lead to what we've been doing here coming out."

His twitch of a smile wasn't appreciated. "No one will find out."

"It's not your life on the line here."

"Your father doesn't want you dead. If he thought you knew anything that could lead to—he'd have done it years ago. Don't you think?"

She stepped closer, lowering her pitch and volume. "My life is nothing compared to those I care about." Yeah, not so funny now. "And if you don't take Gambatto capability seriously, you shouldn't be doing this job."

"He's weak—"

"You think that matters?" Her laugh wasn't one of amusement. "God, all this time and you've learned nothing."

His brow hardened. "I've learned plenty. Most important of which is where the power lies. I could choose to live in fear, put the possibilities ahead of faith that we will come out on top. But I don't. I don't give him the power. He doesn't have it unless you put it in his hands." His scrutiny narrowed. "That's what he wants, can't you see that? Trust your own strength. Otherwise, he wins."

And that sounded exactly like something Breck would say. It must be nice to have that kind of clarity. Every time, in the past, when she'd underestimated the patriarch, she'd lived to regret it.

Damnit, shouldn't it be different by now? Why did she regress to an anxiety-ridden teenager every time she imagined facing off with her father? She was a confident, successful woman, her own strength grew every day.

Pop psychology would have to wait for another time. He'd distracted her long enough.

"Stay here," was all she said and left, without him on her heels.

NINETEEN

IF PORTER WANTED to show up at Roxie's on his own, so be it. They wouldn't be showing up together. Confident, she had nothing to hide, entering Roxie's apartment, she didn't shrink. And sure enough, there were two women in the kitchen holding coffee cups. Roxie and the woman from yesterday. Rainie?

No big deal. "Morning," she said.

Neither woman set any expectation on her.

"Morning," Roxie replied. "You okay?"

"Yeah." She scanned the room. "Tripp around?"

"Still in bed," Roxie said. "We think. Who knows with him? He could be chasing tail in China by now."

Porter had suggested Roxie may disappear into the night, but Roxie was right in her assertion too. Tripp could find a party anywhere, any city, any state, any country. And he got offers every minute. His life moved with the wind, he went wherever appealed most in any given moment.

Only one way to find out whether he was still in the building. Not that it was him she was really looking for. She left the women to head into the hallway and the bedroom designated Tripp's.

Yep, there he was. Lying on his chest, face buried in the pillow, back bare with the sheet draped across his hips. The sexy, snuggly picture would tempt many women.

Women who weren't her.

And he was just a distraction. Going for her real prize, she snagged the cellphone from its dock and sat on the bed, crossing her legs in front of her before dialing. Rearranging Tripp's hair, she tucked one section under another. Wow, his eyelashes were ridiculously long. How come guys got perks like that? Because they didn't slather them with cosmetics, that was why.

Come on. How long would she wait for the phone to stop ringing?

When it did, she spoke before he could. "That was at least ten rings, Stat. Are you mad at me?"

"I was in the shower."

"Huh, you're the second man I've dragged from the shower today."

How did Tripp get his hair so soft? And that dark brown laced through the honey and caramel hues. Had to be a professional job, didn't it? Maybe, but she couldn't see him sitting in one place long enough for anyone to color his hair.

"Why were you in the shower with Tripp?"

"He isn't the man I was talking about, but I am in bed with him right now."

"At this time of day, that means nothing. He's still unconscious."

Probably not quite, but he definitely hadn't stirred.

"How many women sneak in and out of bed with him all the time? He should install a turnstile. Nothing to worry about. The boy wouldn't know what to do with me even if he tried."

"No, he would not. Are you coming home today?"

Oh, her man, so predictable. "No foreplay? Straight to the climax?"

"Never had a problem with me taking you there before."

"Your brother's in the room, baby. I don't think he'd appreciate waking up to us having phone sex."

"Better your side than his," the guy lying beside her mumbled from the corner of his mouth without moving.

Pushing his head into the pillow, she silenced him and lay down on her side, back to the slumberer.

"Do you have interviews today?"

"That why you called me, Coy?" Breck asked. "To ask about interviews? Worried I'm just lying around watching TV?"

"You deserve some time just laying around." Though nothing would be more foreign to him. "I called because…" She couldn't be forthcoming with certain details, that didn't mean she should hide everything. "You've been with me. I couldn't sleep last night."

"Which only happens when you feel you've left something undone."

"I don't like to leave things undone."

"No, you do not." Neither did he. "So you got up and did it."

"I did."

The reassurance of their familiarity was exactly what she needed. Drawing her knees up, she closed her eyes to bask in the comfort of his voice.

"And with me not there to drag you back, you never returned to bed."

"This is why I love you. You always know what I need."

"You need me, and you left. You left our family."

For then, it might be just them, would it always be that way?

"I'm doing it again," she murmured on a sigh. Falling into him, them, wasn't fair with so much uncertainty hovering. "When will I learn to distance myself?"

"Never. You never have to learn and *we*'re doing it again. We talk to each other like this, rely on each other, because we're in love and building a future."

"We're not supposed to be doing that."

"Stop fighting it, baby. You see any other man in your future?"

Of course she didn't, or this wouldn't be so hard. "I told you, without you, it's blank."

"It will never be blank. You're out there doing what you need to do, I trust you. I'll keep the homestead safe. Whenever you're ready, I'm waiting for you."

"Oh, God," she groaned and rolled onto her back, pressing a fist against her forehead. "Why do you have to say things like that? Stop being romantic. I'm too far away to rip your clothes off."

"My clothes are staying on," came another mumble from Sleeping Beauty beside her.

Damn right they were.

She rolled onto her back, the guy still hadn't even opened his eyes. "No one's talking to you." All she could see was skin anyway, which led to the question... "Are you wearing anything right now?"

"Never wear anything in bed."

"Okay..." she said and sat up, legs dangling from the side. "Your brother is a cretin."

Breck laughed. "You crashed his morning." Good point. "I'm surprised he's alone."

"Not from a lack of desire," she explained. "He was told he could go looking for it. Neither of us were giving it to him."

"Thank God," Tripp's voice may be a little more awake, marginally. "A guy wouldn't make it out alive from that tag team."

"You were told there's a single woman in the building."

"Gwennie? Not so single, she's sleeping with her boss."

Incredulous, his knowing that was both impressive and horrifying. "How do you know that?"

"Ah, too messy for my taste at this time in the morning."

Just as he rolled onto his back to stretch, the bedroom door opened to reveal Roxie.

"Good, you're awake," the hostess said, then pointed at her. "Who's on the phone?"

"Her boyfriend," Tripp answered for her, letting out a bear call in his next stretch. "It's never fun when I wake up to you, Rox Out."

"Because I have the original and you're a cheap imitation."

Tripp opened his arms, flashing a dazzling smile. "New and improved."

"Yeah, in your dreams. You can't improve on perfection."

He laughed. "I'm telling Zairn you said he was perfect."

"He'll never believe you. Besides, I molded him into what he is today."

"Faithful?"

"Among other things. His perfection is Roxie-induced. And you're welcome."

Zairn had never been the type to screw around. Keep his options open in his younger days? Sure. But he was honest about it. That was a long time ago. Relatively speaking. And he'd always been a decent, honorable man, some things were engrained.

Breck hadn't said anything for a while.

"You still there, Stat?"

"Still here."

"I should go and figure out what's next with these guys."

"Always here if you need me." Yes, he was. "I love you."

"I know you do," she teased and hung up.

"Ah, young love," Roxie said.

Instead of staring at the phone, she should get moving, time was running short.

"I have to be back at work on Monday," she said. "Can I get a ride to the airport?"

"You know it's only Saturday," Roxie said, climbing onto the end of the bed to sit with them as she drew her bent knees back up. "You don't have to rush back to Manhattan."

"I'm not rushing back. I have another stop to make."

"Oh, another stop…" Roxie drew nearer. "Let me guess, it begins with L and ends in A." When she tilted her head, Roxie just shrugged. "Might not seem like it, but I do pay attention." She poked Tripp's leg, still concealed under the sheet. "Want to join us in the sun, Priest?"

"Crimson Isle?" He was right there, no way he hadn't heard their previous exchange. "I never say no to California."

"Because there are so many babes in micro-mini skirts flashing their boobs?"

"No, just love the hot dogs."

"Okay, but we can't stay at Lilya's. The house is being renovated before they bring the baby back."

"We have options," Tripp said. "But, so we're clear, if you get arrested, Rox Out, I'm not bailing you out. My mom doesn't need to see that picture on the internet."

"All the crazy pictures of you out there, and this is where you draw the line?"

Tripp drew a line on the bed with a fingertip. "Right there..." But when he licked his lips, his smile reigned. "'Cause I've got to say, you leaving Z at the altar because you're locked up... there's poetry in that."

Rather than be offended, Roxie laughed. "Oh, the things you don't know, little one."

"Now I'm intrigued."

"Be intrigued," she said and leaped to her feet. "But do it on the way to the airport."

TWENTY

"I SHOULD'VE ASKED…" she said, drawing her attention away from LA passing beyond the car window. "Was Zairn mad we left New York?"

"I don't know," Roxie replied. "I didn't ask him."

"You couldn't tell by talking to him?"

"Casanova knows to expect the unexpected from me. He likes it when I let loose," Roxie said, adjusting her angle until her whole body aimed her way. The position matched the expectation on the beauty's brow. "And since we're asking questions, do you want to tell us where you disappeared to last night?"

"I didn't disappear last night, I… I went out this morning to get my head straight."

"Uh huh. Out where?"

"Nowhere specific, just wandering."

"You weren't wearing shoes… or pants." Yeah, and there was the flaw in her plan. She'd only been wearing the tee-shirt Roxie provided for her to sleep in. No idea who it belonged to, but she'd guess the owner was male. What a great idea, Porter, so much for Roxie accepting a non-answer. "You don't answer to anyone, honey, but this is a safe space, right here. We won't report back to your guy, no matter what."

Is that what Roxie thought? That she'd been out looking for action?

Roxie's foot sprang out to catch Tripp on the shin even though the rest of her didn't move.

"What? Ow," Tripp said, barely lowering his phone. No way that subtle kick was hard enough to hurt. "I don't promise silence, it comes as standard. But you're crazy if you think she let any other guy touch her."

"You may have a vested interest in believing your brother gets the prize," Roxie said, addressing the man still typing into his phone. "Around here we keep our options open. And if someone wants to take a different path, we support them, without judgment."

That was almost funny.

"He's a Breckenridge," Sequoia said, beaming in pride and amusement. "They're taught support not judgment before they can walk." Roxie sighed and sank against the backrest. "You're right. I wasn't walking. I can't tell you where I was, but it wasn't a betrayal. Breck would support me."

If she ever told him.

"Support not judgment," Tripp muttered then groaned and raised his phone before dropping his hand to his lap. "If we're in a three-way cellphone situation, the least you two could do is provide a charger."

"Blame Z for that, he's always hiding them from me. Don't worry, youngster, the world can do without us for a while."

"I'm older than you," Tripp said.

"Yet not quite ripe. You still have some growing to do, honey."

His swagger bloomed. "I grow and show, honey."

Sheesh, her eyes rolled. Who was he trying to impress?

Roxie hunkered her head lower. "It's exciting being disconnected from the world, a little scary, exhilarating."

"Yeah, for you. You live for giving your guy a heart attack every once in a while," Tripp said, shaking the phone at Roxie. "Some of us have lives to run."

"Oh, you are not on there boosting your portfolio or making time-sensitive corporate choices. You're lining up tonight's pussy."

He sniffed. "I'm getting withdrawal."

"You're not the only one," Roxie said and their eyes met.

Both shivered and spoke together, "Never."

LA offered hope and confusion, this trip was supposed to level her life. What if she failed? What if she couldn't—it didn't matter, she had to try.

"I got them to bring things to the hotel," Roxie said. "Clothes from the plane, Lilya's place—or wherever. Point is, everything we need will be waiting for us."

"Thank you," she said. "You didn't have to come with me, I would've figured this out..."

"Tripp and I love an adventure."

"Yeah, but you're getting married and—"

"Jane's taking care of all that. Details."

Would she be so glib about her own wedding? Yeah, right, like that would happen any time soon. A woman like Roxie, popular, in the public eye, people wanted to see it, they wanted the spectacle of ice sculptures and swans and all the trimmings. Except what she'd learned about the woman spoke to her sincerity. That frivolity was expected by the masses, and Roxie would give the crowd what they wanted. Even if it was her best friend organizing the whole thing.

"Are you nervous?"

"About what?" Roxie asked, completely relaxed. "Going to the hotel? I've been here before. In fact, if you're in the mood for a little nostalgia, Zairn and I met in this hotel."

"You did?"

"Yeah," Roxie said and the glimpse of a secret smile endeared her even further. "A long time ago."

"How long ago?"

"A year, year and a half. Something like that." Roxie sighed. "Sometimes it's like we met yesterday..." The woman's eyes narrowed. "But I can't remember not being in love with him."

"Which is funny, 'cause you couldn't stand the guy when you met," Tripp added. "Must've been sexual tension."

"Uh, no, not sexual tension, he was rude." Roxie didn't equivocate. "He came storming in there like—no way would I put up with that. Everyone else might let him get away with it. Not me. I did nothing wrong and he had no right to talk to me like he did."

"You gave it back though."

"I stood my ground, still do if the occasion calls for it."

"Ah, come on, admit it, you just do it to turn him on."

"Hey..." Roxie muttered, eyes slinking to their corners. "It's not the kinkiest thing he's asked me to do."

And as the day flashed past outside, she saw the woman in a different light. "You suit him. Zairn. He's always been looking for something," she said. "I didn't know it, but... you suit him."

"He was looking for something; I didn't know I was looking." On an exhale, Roxie conceded. "If it wasn't for him getting it, us, so early, we wouldn't have made it at all."

She clarified her earlier question. "Are you nervous about getting married?"

"Married?" Roxie was certain. "Never think about it, to be honest. Z and I do events together all the time. This is no different, not really. It means a lot to Jane, I'm excited to see her happy."

"But the dress, the crowd—"

"There's a prize at the end," Roxie said. "That's more than we usually get. We've never cared too much about the wedding part, we care about the marriage. We're good at that; we like being good at things. Let's us be smug."

"It'll be a sight to see," Tripp said. "Big fanfare. Pulling out all the stops. Real theater."

And he was a guy with options.

"Who are you taking as your date, Tripp?" she asked him. "Did you get a plus-twelve? A plus-twenty?"

"Can't play favorites. I'm going stag, but I can get you in," Tripp teased, making her smile. "I know a guy."

"Yeah, your brother." Roxie seemed concerned. "You're not coming with Breck? Asshole. We'll uninvite him and you can take his place, Sequoia. There it's done. If he shows up, he'll be tossed out on his ass."

"Be warned." Tripp feigned solemnity. "You'll have to go through security to get in there, Seq."

"Don't worry about that. Wait until you see Roux's dress. Every man in the building will be distracted." Roxie's lips circled. "Whoa, mama, there's a definite chance of fireworks."

"She didn't get to make fireworks at her own wedding, so she's commandeering yours?" Tripp did his insight into women thing again. "Nice."

"Hey, she's welcome to it. Only spotlight I need is my Casanova's. Of course..." One of Roxie's shoulders rose an inch, "Jane may not say the same thing."

The last thing she wanted to do was cause upset. "Breck and I haven't talked about your wedding. Don't uninvite him."

Tripp had the answer. "Guarantee he assumes you're going with him."

She shrugged. "Probably."

"He wouldn't take anyone else."

No, he wouldn't. Until meeting Roxie, and having this whole experience, she hadn't thought about the hyped wedding, or if she wanted to go. Tripp was right though, she and Breck did automatically assume the other would be their plus-one, if required. Damn, she'd have to get a dress in case he presented the prospect last minute.

"Okay, he can come, but as your plus-one." Satisfied, Roxie's lips curled. "Problem solved."

"New York will be empty that weekend," Tripp added. "Think there'll be looting?"

"I already said details are Jane's purview. But don't worry, I'm sure your harem will be suitably distraught."

"No different from any other day they're without me." What a dork. "I'm surprised everyone will fit in LA. Are we renting out soundstages? Offering complimentary silk sleeping bags and scented eye masks?"

What would be the point of scenting an eye mask?

"More details," Roxie said, her hand sweeping away the concept. "Think less about me and more about you. I'm betting you don't have a room reserved anywhere. Where will you sleep, Breckenridge?"

"Ah…" In typical Tripp fashion, he wasn't fussed. "It'll work itself out."

"Always land on your feet, don't you, boy." And that was one of the things she loved about Tripp, everyone loved about him, worrying just wasn't in his nature. "Someone's bound to be brokenhearted, right?"

"Hey, now, I don't only hit the easy prey. I wait for it to come to me. I have to be available, in case an emergency arises."

They laughed. "Won't be the only thing arising, I'll bet." Roxie smoothed her skirt. "Your mom will be there, don't forget that."

"Ah, the old ones leave early, plenty of time late into the night for the real party."

Weddings. When with Breck, she thought about it. Hell, whether they were officially together or not, she'd often considered how their nuptials might go.

Breck wouldn't have much of an opinion, he'd like whatever she liked because color schemes and flower arrangements weren't high on his priority list. In the past, at least. Maybe now he was unemployed and unoccupied, he'd want the distraction.

Ha, what a giggle, could she really see him getting particular over place cards and chair silks? No. Was there such a thing as a groomzilla?

Shit, and she was doing it again. *Again.* There wouldn't be a wedding, not any time soon. Assumptions like that, imaginings, daydreams, they were how she ended up hurting herself, pining for an uncertain future. And why they got caught up in each other, forgetting that others existed.

"Are you having the reception at Crimson?" she asked to get back to the point.

Roxie's wedding. Not her wedding.

"Drinks reception before and after at the hotel, and they're catering for us." Roxie inhaled. "I think, anyway. But, yeah, Crimson into the night. It's great to pre-own a gargantuan space."

"Not much different to every other day of the week." Tripp slid lower in his seat. "Cam coming?"

"I think he's already in town. Some project, something. Miss him?"

"He's the only one of the Colliers I understand."

Roxie's burst of laughter startled her. "You understand Cam Collier? You? Give me a break. You'd combust in three seconds flat if you made the commitment he did."

"Does he know we're in town?" she asked, struck by a glimmer of panic. "Does Cam know?"

"Because if Cam knows, Caspian knows." Yes, the two Collier brothers probably talked to each other. Tripp translated, taking her thought to its conclusion. "And Caspian will talk to Breck."

"Breck doesn't know we're in LA?" Roxie asked. "If he wants to show up, he can. Doesn't mean he'll be allowed to see you if you don't want him to see you."

"It's not that, it's..."

"Caspian Collier is one of Breck's best friends. They talk, probably every day," Tripp explained. Yes, thank you. "So if we need something fixing..."

"Talking about understanding Colliers. Caspian's one of the few people in the world I don't understand." Roxie folded her arms. "He's so... impervious."

Tripp added. "He has a one-track mind."

"So do you," both she and Roxie said together.

"Yeah, but my track is fun and interesting, his track is more... corporate. Way less fun."

"Heavy is the head..." she muttered.

Caspian was the eldest of the three Collier brothers. Knox was the middle child, and the only one currently involved with a partner, as far as she knew. Cam was the youngest, yet the most real of the siblings.

"Knox lives a life not too different from yours," Roxie said to Tripp. "Zipping around all over the place."

"Yeah, he lived like that before Jane. Now when he zips, it's in her wake."

That truth warmed Roxie's smile again. "Why do you think I allow him to be with my incredible best friend? If he didn't value how amazing and addictive she is, and prove it time and again, we would never have let him get so close to her. Jane's precious, a gem of a human being. She deserves more than the world."

"Rox Out is protective of her girls," Tripp explained.

Yes, she'd heard as much. "Loyalty is a valuable commodity."

"It's nice to meet a person who appreciates that." Roxie straightened as the car rolled to a stop. "Time to settle in."

TWENTY-ONE

THEY DIDN'T GET MUCH time to relax before their assigned butler came into the suite to announce a guest.

"A guest?" she asked as the butler went to fetch them. "Who knows we're here?"

"Since Roxie landed?" Tripp inhaled. "Everyone."

Huh, maybe it wasn't such a great idea to travel with a celebrity when attempting to go under the radar. Especially when visiting a city that was all about fame, faces, and who's who. Everyone was paying attention there. Many people would want to get near Roxie, especially so close to the wedding.

Except when their guest came striding in, he wasn't any autograph hunter.

"Bastian," she breathed.

Uh oh.

Something she hadn't mentioned? Breck had more than one close friend. He had two. Men he'd entrust with his life, or hers, brothers in every way that counted: Caspian Collier and Bastian Hunt.

Maybe "brothers" wasn't the right descriptor. Part of the appeal was them being out of the Breckenridge stratosphere. Yes, the three families interacted, but each of the three men understood what it was to be relied on heavily. Being the eldest of their generation, they assumed the responsibility of sustaining their families and perpetuating the legacy. It was no wonder they had such an affinity.

While she'd been busy worrying about workaholic Caspian Collier, she hadn't considered the other guy living in town. Not just living in town, he owned the hotel they were standing in, this one and the rest of them. She'd stayed in Grand Hotels plenty and never come across him. Of course it would be the one time she wanted privacy that he'd pop up right where she was.

"Seq," Bastian said, his welcoming smile so bright she couldn't regret him being there.

When he opened his arms, she went into them. It was an odd relief to have them close around her. Nothing would go wrong now. Not until she stepped out of the hug anyway.

He and Tripp shook hands. "Good to see you, man." When their hands dropped, Roxie got everyone's attention. "Have you met Roxie?"

"No, which is a wonder, given you're getting married here soon."

"Do you have a rule about meeting every couple marrying in your hotels?" Roxie asked.

"When they're booking out the entire hotel, and all our sister hotels in the area, I should," Bastian said. "You're single-handedly funding our expansion." He offered a hand. "Bastian Hunt."

"Roxanna Kyst." Though apparently dubious, Roxie gave him her hand to shake. "I know your mother."

"Yes, and she speaks highly of you. Incredibly highly. No Zairn?"

"Not yet. I'm sure he'll show up before the big day. If not, we'll draw another guy's name from a hat. Someone will stand up with me. Our deposits are non-refundable anyway, you have nothing to worry about."

"Bastian's a good guy," Tripp said, bumping Roxie's arm with his. "Stop busting his balls."

"Are you married, Mr. Hunt?" Roxie asked him, seeming reluctant to trust Tripp's claim, if she'd even heard it.

"No."

"Girlfriend?"

"No. Are you interested in the role? I thought you were getting married. I may have to refund the deposits if we run away together, Ms. Kyst."

The tease was meant to ease the mood. Tripp was right, Bastian was a good guy.

"No girlfriend?" Tripp made a sound. "Put Robyn back on the market?"

"Yes, feel free to take a swing."

"Oh, no thank you, man, I like my balls where they are. How'd that go down?"

"Mutually. We finished it."

"Wow, that was overdue."

Bastian laughed. "Thanks."

"No offense, man, but she's a praying mantis."

"And I made it out alive, can't ask for anything more." He landed his gaze on her. "Seq, you have a minute to talk?"

Oh, this wouldn't be good. Was the riot act by proxy heading her way?

"Sure."

She hadn't done anything reckless or dangerous. Okay, maybe swanning into Chicago without a SWAT team could be deemed reckless—depending on the onlooker's perspective—but Roxie had security, that was enough.

They went into the master bedroom and Bastian actually closed the door. Oh, yeah, whatever was coming, she'd have to brace for impact.

"Breck didn't mention you were coming into town."

"He didn't know." Probably did now, because it was unlikely Bastian hadn't called him. "You didn't have to come all the way over here—"

"I was in the building already," he said, concern etched on his brow. "Why wouldn't you want me to visit?"

"I didn't say I wouldn't want you to visit. I'm happy to see you, I just... was hoping to slip in quietly."

"Because you're here to do something Breck doesn't approve of?"

"Have you heard...?" Of course he had. "Breck quit the company."

"Yeah. Haven't got to the bottom of it yet."

Surrendering, she went to sit in one of the soft seats by the window. "He's doing it for me—for us."

He came to join her, taking the angled armchair beside hers. "You asked him to quit?"

"No! Why would I ask him to do that? I knew nothing about it. Not until after the fact. I had to hunt him down to learn what he'd done." Yeah, on that note, she'd have to ask Breck exactly when he'd planned to tell her. "He says he's doing it for us."

"Because you were always worried your father would take advantage of the Breckenridge connection. So Breck severed it." With an exhale, his concern relaxed. "Well that makes more sense of it."

"No, it does not!" She stopped just short of punching the side of her fist against the chair's arm. "It's ridiculous. I never wanted him to walk away from

Breckenridge. This whole damn mess is my fault. Why didn't he talk to me about it first? Before doing something so crazy?"

"Probably because he knew he'd give in when you asked him to stay. He always gives in to you."

"Not this time. This time he's adamant he's getting a minimum wage job. He'll end up a smiling barista, small talking it up with the shiny, happy customers."

He laughed. "Do you really see that?"

"No, but I... I don't know how—he'll never be happy in this life. Breckenridge is everything to him, the job, his family, it's his identity. It's who he is. He lives to be relied upon. Has huge pride in... The money isn't what matters, it's the belonging. He needs to belong."

"You matter to him more than anything else."

Did he have to be so sentimental? "Do you know what it's like to have something done in your name without ever having a say in how it came about?"

"Is that why you're here? Putting distance between you? Did you finish it?"

"We finish every other week, you know that. We weren't even together when he did this. We didn't talk or... I can't let his life spiral. I can't."

"So what's your plan? Stay away from New York until he gives up on you and moves on?" His brow moved a fraction. "Because you know he won't. He won't move on. You've got to know how he feels about you—I know you know it. Every guy who's ever seen you two together knows it and hates you both for making it look so easy."

When his smile returned, she managed a feeble response. Okay, maybe a tiny smidge of sentimentality was allowed.

"I love him."

"And he loves you. What happened to having a

baby?"

"Oh, God," she groaned. "He told you too? What does that man not understand about private? He's the most private guy there is, but this he blabs everywhere?"

"Because he's proud of you," Bastian said on a snicker, "and the future he wants with you. Why should he keep that a secret?"

"Future. Future. Future. Everything's always about the future. Meanwhile, there's my father, looming large, just waiting for me to take the Breckenridge name. I know it. I know him. That's what he's waiting for. It feels like everyone's just holding their breath. This whole space, distance, thing is a con. He wants us to believe he's forgotten about me and Breck, that he doesn't care. I guarantee he does. About himself, yes, and his interests. When it comes to either of those things, he's all about the caring and paying attention."

"Breck wouldn't let him hurt you."

"It's not me I'm worried about. I've lived with it, I know how to handle it. I'd never visit that on the Breckenridges. Can you imagine anything worse? They're such a good, kind family."

Why did she have any right to be a part of something so pure and virtuous? More of that Gambatto selfishness shone through. Her blood shouldn't poison theirs. It wouldn't be right. Why couldn't she help herself?

"The Breckenridges care about you, they love you. They wouldn't want you to think you're alone in this. You're not alone in this. It's okay to rely on others, to take help when it's offered. Wouldn't you help someone you cared about?"

Yes, and he knew that. Giving was so much easier than taking. This wasn't as simple as helping someone move to a new apartment. This situation could actually come with physical harm. Others were ignorant to that; it was on her to defuse the risk. Or walk away.

"I'm the only one who can fix it," she said, "who can make a difference and protect them from being exploited."

"How? How do you plan to do that?"

Oh, she could fib, she could hide and cower, but this was Bastian. Not trusting him was impossible. She'd seen him with his sister, with his mother, with the Breckenridges.

His consideration was so genuine, it was intoxicating.

And, as anticipated, this was where the need to brace kicked in. "I spoke to the prosecutor in Chicago."

There. It was out.

Instantly, he starched his spine and furrowed that brow. "You're going to testify?"

"No! No. I was very clear about that. I just gave him... a nudge or two."

"What did Breck say when you—you haven't told him, have you?"

Yeah, he probably got that from her wincing cringe. "I need him to be safe."

"He thinks the same thing about you. Jesus, Seq, what if something had happened to you?"

No need to overreact. "We were in Chicago one night. I'm here. I'm fine."

"Everything I heard about Roxanna suggested—I can't believe Tripp let you do this."

When he grabbed for the arms of the chair as though he intended to get up, she lunged over to snatch his hand and stop him.

"He didn't know, doesn't know, neither of them do. Not that I gave the ADA anything. They were there when I met the prosecutor at first, they thought I just wanted to ask questions about the chances of success."

"Of imprisoning your father. Because you

believe if he's in jail, you're free to be with Breck." When she shrugged, he sighed. "You went and saw this ADA again? Alone?"

"He lives in the same building we stayed in, he's Roxie's ex. I didn't go to his office, I wasn't seen with him. I was safe. But, yeah, I went down there to..."

"Nudge him." Hmm, disapproval, but not exactly judgment. "What's done is done. But you're not finished, are you? You think there's more to do here? What's LA got to do with it?"

"My brother Joey killed Dayah Lynn, the actress." According to Trish and that was enough for her. "Murdered her." That was such shock news, he deserved a beat or two to process it. "The DA here is invested. Heavily invested."

"Ackley, I know him, he's dedicated." Hopefully to the truth. "You want to nudge him too? Where? Nudge him toward what? Your father is a Chicago problem, is he not?"

"The plan with him is slightly different... It's complicated though, Ackley and Roxie have history."

"Yes. Given the way Zairn was treated after Dayah's death, it doesn't surprise me there's acrimony there."

"That was long before he and Roxie got together..." Long? Maybe not so long. Memory could teach valuable lessons. "Roxie's not Ackley's biggest fan and the feeling is mutual." From what she could gather. "So I need to figure out a way I can get to him without Roxie thinking she has to come along."

"Because if you show up with her, Ackley won't be receptive to what you have to say."

Bingo. "I don't want to insult Roxie. She's been incredible, kind, generous, she's supported me, even when we were practically strangers."

The woman had been with her when she read the

negative pregnancy test, one of the most profound moments of her life.

"And she can support you in this too, from the sidelines."

That would be the hope, but she didn't want to tell the woman she wasn't welcome when she'd done so much.

Bastian sighed. "I'll make a call; we'll go see him tomorrow."

Uh, hold up. "We?" That hadn't been her intention at all. "You don't need to come. Breck doesn't know about any of this, and I don't want to put you in the middle. You shouldn't have to lie to him for me."

"Do you have any idea what he would do to me if he discovered I'd walked away from you? What my mother would do?" That last question came with a smile that quickly faded. "Ackley's paranoid about his own safety. He travels with security who won't let you near him. I can get you in without any fuss, without an explanation. Do you want to explain to security and assistants why it's important you talk to him? Remembering, of course, we're in one of the most paparazzi-infested cities in the world."

And there it was. Nuts. "The price for your help is your attendance?"

"Yep."

She knew him well enough to know he wouldn't budge. "Okay, but you can't tell Breck. He'll talk you out of it." He nodded once. "Will Ackley meet us on a Sunday?"

"I can make it Monday, if you'd prefer."

"No, it can't be Monday, it has to be this weekend. I have to work on Monday."

"Benedict Breckenridge won't deny you some personal time. He'd never deny you anything." Bastian stood up. "Either way, Sunday or Monday, Ackley may want a follow up meeting. I'd plan on being in LA for a few days at least."

"I can't take advantage of Ben's kindness."

"You never ask that family for anything. I promise you he won't mind. Give him a call before I take you to dinner."

A call? No, a text would need less explanation... Tripp would need a phone charger.

Bastian offered a hand and she took it, allowing him to help her to her feet. "I don't want to leave Roxie and Tripp—"

"I'm taking all of you out for a meal. And you can repay the favor by getting me into Roxanna's good graces. My mother may disown me if I don't have her approval."

"Why is she giving you a hard time?"

"No idea, but I'd like it to stop."

"Okay. Is there somewhere in town that does good deep dish?"

Dinner was dinner, and she was hungry. The least she could do was help him out with Roxie. Ben would give her time off, of course, but it would raise questions. Her boss may not press for details, but his wife, his son...? Could be she'd face her own hard time in the not-too-distant future.

TWENTY-TWO

TURNED OUT BASTIAN'S presence helped when leaving the hotel suite in the morning. His company gave her a reason to request Tripp and Roxie stay behind. They couldn't barrel into Ackley's office like a posse. A show of force wouldn't win her any grace. And, to be honest, the fewer people who knew what she intended to say, the better.

Her hands were clammy; her fingers wouldn't stay still. It wasn't nerves, she'd been in plenty of high stakes meetings. She could keep her cool, be articulate, persuasive—this wasn't just high stakes. This was forever. This meeting could dictate the rest of her life. Not just hers. Breck's, his whole family's. It could be the difference between them having a child, and her giving up on the idea for good.

In Chicago, she may not have known the reason for their destination until it was upon her, but Roxie had personal capital with Porter. Like love and affection type capital. If he'd shot her down or tried to kick her out, Roxie could've stepped in. With Ackley? She didn't have the same safety net. She couldn't fuck this up.

"I've never seen you anxious," Bastian said from her side as they strode down the marble floored hallway.

Yeah, uh huh, because that was a helpful observation.

"I'm not anxious." Clenching her fists, she pulled back control. "There's a lot riding on this."

"Have you spoken to Breck?"

"Not yet." There was nothing to tell. Nothing more than she'd known that morning or yesterday. Though she'd feel better right then if he was holding her hand. Which she couldn't complain about because it was on her that he wasn't present. "I told you he doesn't need to know about this."

"He said your phone is off."

Stopping suddenly, she caught him almost off-guard by body-blocking him to a halt too. "You've spoken to him? When? If you told him you saw me—"

"Yesterday, before I knew you were in town," Bastian said, the picture of calm. "He told me yesterday your phone was off. Which is something he said you only do when you don't want him to know your location."

"Did you tell him? That I'm here?"

"No, but if he knows you're with Roxie, the world knows where she is."

Yeah, she'd been trying not to focus on that. Damn her conversation with him in Tripp's bed.

"I'm with Tripp, I'm safe, he knows his brother won't abandon me. Breck will give me time to figure this out."

He'd said as much, though hadn't put a number on just how much he'd give.

Bastian frowned. "Wouldn't it be easier just to turn off the tracker?"

"That makes no difference when he knows the man who designed the phone." She started walking again. "My guy can be overbearing."

He ducked a little, still in stride with her. "Protective. It's a sign of love."

"So I'm told. Do you say the same thing to Keely?"

He laughed. "All the time."

"Poor girl."

His sister was anything but poor, in every sense of the word. Yet she was also one of the kindest, most dynamic women she'd ever met.

In the middle of the corridor, she stopped again, this time to face the doors that would take her to Ackley. Time for business…

"Do I have to remind you that you don't have to be in this?" she said to the man at her side. Focused straight ahead, her scrutiny zeroed in on the handles that would grant her access. "Get me in and then you can walk away."

"Haven't forgotten and I'm not going anywhere."

Nope, of course not, these billionaires could be audacious to the point of rude.

"Promise me this won't change anything."

"I thought changing things was the idea," he said, concern creeping in. "If you've changed your mind—"

"No, I know what I have to do." She glanced at him. "I don't want it to change things between us." Ackley could tell her to go to hell and Breck would never know what had been said. Except if Bastian was right next to her, hearing every word, she couldn't deny the truth. "I value our friendship."

"As do I," he said and took her hand to kiss the back of it, locking their fingers together. "And you'll always have it."

"Okay." One nod. "Let's do this."

Passing through the doors, into a busy bullpen of

cubicles, the offices left and right contained people too, everyone lost in the importance of their business. Should it be so busy on a Sunday? Didn't these people take any time off? Maybe it was a case of, if the boss was in, everyone was in.

At the other side of the space were double doors. Solid, private, concealing what went on inside. Bastian guided her around the room to those doors. Without waiting he went inside and closed them in.

Quiet. The rumble of business they'd just left still hummed behind the wood, but it wasn't intrusive. Privacy, maybe, hopefully, went both ways.

Bastian released her hand to continue the couple of steps to a desk occupied by a woman wearing a headset, fingers poised over the keyboard like they'd interrupted her mid-strike.

"Dierdra." The warmth of Bastian's voice betrayed his smile. "How are you doing?"

"Well, Mr. Hunt. He's eager for this meeting."

Huh, maybe she should've asked exactly what Bastian said to get them in.

"That's nice to hear," Bastian said. "It's always nice to be welcome."

As she rose from her seat, Dierdra laughed, a light flirtatious sound Bastian probably heard everywhere. Sure, the woman was probably twenty years older than him, but did that ever matter?

"You're always welcome," the assistant said and retreated to another set of double doors. Dierdra knocked once, then, without waiting for a response from inside, opened one of the doors.

Bastian's arm rose as he twisted her way, calling for her to go first, or at least with him into the room beyond.

Shit. It was nerves. No way of denying that now. With an exhale, she went to Bastian, walking with him, his hand on the small of her back. The touch was comforting, but it didn't slow her speeding heart. Adrenaline got her over the threshold.

Breck. He's who mattered. He was what she had to hold onto. Nothing that could happen in that room, or any other, would change how he felt about her... right?

"Bastian!" Ackley, a tall man with a tan and graying hair with flecks of white at the temples, came around to shake his hand. "I hear there's a matter we have to discuss."

"Yes." Bastian's hand strengthened in time with Ackley's focus landing on her. "My friend has important business. I'll let her introduce herself."

Right, because they hadn't spoken about how much of her identity she wanted revealed up front. Did she want her heritage flagged at the head of this meeting? Yes, because everything hinged on her credibility. Were Gambattos credible? In a room like this, for the most part? No, they wouldn't be. But Ackley had to believe her words carried weight, that she was more than just a passerby.

Funny for how many years she'd done everything in her power to conceal her identity, and there she was, ready to declare it to a man with the power to dismantle her whole life.

"Mr. Ackley," she said, edging just a little closer as her shoulders pushed back to hold her confidence. "I'm Sequoia Gambatto."

The flare of his nostrils was the first hint of surprise. He didn't immediately say anything. No, he'd need time to process. Men like him, confident public figures always had something to say and always assumed to be right.

Porter Clement, a Chicagoan, elbow deep in a case involving her family, might immediately recognize her, and even he hadn't. Ackley had no reason to know who she was at all, he may not know she existed.

"A sister," he murmured, surprise becoming intrigue.

Ackley backed off to gesture at the chairs facing his desk as he went around to his grand red, leather chair. This was LA, the city of sleek and modern, Ackley may buy into that at home, he didn't in his office. Broad desk, bookcases behind, flags, this was the full deal. Thank God she wasn't easily intimidated.

"Thank you for seeing us on a Sunday," she said, holding onto her assuredness while projecting respect. Soften up the ground, be sure, not pushy. Not yet. "It's short notice, you couldn't have expected us."

"Bastian said he had a friend who needed my attention, deserved my attention. I could never have predicted this." He glanced between them. "You're a long way from Chicago, Ms. Gambatto. To what do I owe the pleasure?"

Smart, also not presumptuous, could be an act.

"I did travel from Chicago, but I don't live there. I live in New York; my relationship with my father was severed years ago."

"Intriguing, rather than whet my appetite, she tempers my expectation." This meeting was for her, yet he spoke to Bastian. Was it about gender? Money? Familiarity? "Are you here to ask for something, or give me something?"

Had to be one of those two, huh? Probably what he was used to, and in his defense, he was right.

"Does it have to be one or the other? Why can't we do both?"

"Now she's whetting my appetite. What would you like to give me?"

Okay, not overtly sleazy, but there was an undertone. Could be her imagination. Though bringing

Bastian was working in her favor. Was she scared of Ackley? No. But she appreciated the witness all the same.

"My father."

And his scrutiny narrowed. "Has he committed a crime?"

"Several."

"In my city?"

"That's for you to decide."

"Okay," he said, reaching for the laptop on the corner of the desk.

"No," she was quick to object. "This is all off the record."

His hand splayed on the desk. "Off the record? That's of no use to me."

"Maybe you should hear what I have to say first. My brother, I know, is in your sights. Trish makes that case for you."

"She's willing to testify."

"Why don't you hear what Sequoia has to say first?" Bastian was nothing if not a great mediator. "There could be irrefutable evidence. Maybe you don't need her testimony."

Now, with a hint of adversity in the air, this wasn't seeming like such a great idea. He could tell her to get out, that he planned to do nothing. Wouldn't be the first time a DA, or other official, had been paid off. Ackley could be in her father's pocket, which put her in a precarious position. Risk was part of the plan; it had to be. The potential reward at the end, if everything went their way, was worth tiptoeing into the lion's den. Confident? Yes. But careful.

"There's evidence. Only depends how hungry you are, Mr. Ackley. My testimony won't hold much sway. As I said, I haven't been close to my father for a long time. That doesn't mean I'm unaware of his methods, his avenues of escape."

"Communicating with your sister has been difficult. She prefers to work through a third party." Probably Zairn. "She hasn't offered us anything on your father's relationship with my city."

"Maybe after today, she'll be more receptive."

"Is she aware of what you're doing here?"

"No one except the three of us are aware of this meeting or what I have to share," she said. "My father disperses his money throughout the country. He's particularly proud of how he uses LA to legitimize his funds. And he's not the only one. Three men work together: him and two others. Catch one, you'll catch them all."

"A conspiracy?" he said and she acknowledged the question with a nod. "And you have details?"

"I'm not completely out of the loop, Mr. Ackley. I can have value without standing up in court."

"I could subpoena you."

"Yes, and I'd plead the fifth for every question, which won't strengthen your case."

"Why would you do that? Because you're involved?"

"Because the last thing I want is to be involved. I give you my father... for a cost."

"Ah," Ackley said, pushing back in his chair. "The quid pro quo. You have a friend in one of my facilities? Need something expunged from a record?"

Did he really expect her to ask for a favor like that? What kind of people did he deal with every day? Probably best not to ask; this was as close to the criminal element as she ever wanted to get again.

"I'll give you the information, and no matter what happens in Chicago, you promise to pursue this."

"Until I have the information, I can't make any promise." Confusion edged in. "That's what you want in return? Your father prosecuted?"

"I want him in a place that he can't hurt anyone anymore. I don't believe in miracles or lucky breaks, I believe in forward-planning, anticipating the unexpected. I like to have a backup plan where possible. You are my backup plan, Mr. Ackley.

"My father is dangerous and he's resourceful. Don't underestimate him. He's been running illegal money through your city for years, laughing at people like you because you're oblivious. Do you want him and his friends laughing at you?"

That hit the mark. Appealing to the man's pride got his cooperation, how predictable.

Ackley bristled. "Tell me what you know."

Good, his interest was encouraging. DA Ackley was a man who held a grudge, if Roxie and Zairn's experience was any indicator. It wouldn't be so bad if he developed one toward her father.

"Have you heard of a production company called Enter Out?" she asked.

"No."

"Then let me enlighten you."

TWENTY-THREE

"I'LL BE FINE," she said to Bastian just outside the suite door.

"It's been a long day." He rubbed her arm. "I can stay, or you can come to the house. Mom would love to have you."

The last thing she needed was well-intentioned people fussing.

"No. Thank you. I appreciate the offer, and send her my love, but you've done plenty."

"I wasn't the one swinging the bat," he said, addressing her with pride rather than the expected revulsion. "You surprised Ackley and that's not an easy thing to do."

"I told the truth."

"All these years you've known… Now that you've shared what you know, will there be retribution?"

"Not if no one mentions my name." She started to turn, then thought twice. "Look, like I said in the meeting, this is a backup plan. Chicago might put my father away. If they don't, I want LA waiting in the wings.

And, truthfully, Ackley's only one part of that. They've kept Enter Out off law enforcement's radar for a long time."

"Your father's associates won't be pleased to fall under suspicion because of their connection to him."

"No. They won't."

"Okay." He leaned in to kiss her head. "Stick with Roxie and her security."

"I will."

"And you may not appreciate the suggestion—"

"I'll call Breck."

His smile grew. "Thank you."

She slipped into the suite and closed the door, pausing just a moment to catch her breath. It was surreal. On going to the DA's office, she had every intention of dishing up her father on a silver platter. That wasn't the surreal part, or even what bothered her, that was what came next. It could actually happen, actually work, there was a real possibility she didn't have to be afraid anymore. Not of her father or the family, she'd never feared them for herself, but there was a distinct possibility she could let go of the fear that her father might hurt the Breckenridges.

Except she was scared to hope. This might seem like progress, but it wouldn't be the first time her father pulled a rabbit from his hat at the eleventh hour. If he beat her this time... the consequences for all of them...

Ackley had been open to it. Seemed more optimistic with every word she uttered. It could happen.

Before making any final decisions, she'd have to tell Breck everything. That would be a fun conversation.

"Who's out there?"

Roxie's calling from the living room curled her lips. Pushing away from the door, she traversed the foyer to join her friend. Sitting on the couch with her feet propped on the coffee table, the TV was playing on mute while Roxie blew toward the hot pink varnish on her toenails.

But the color wasn't the biggest shock, not the color of her nails anyway.

"You changed your hair."

Shaking her head, Roxie ran a hand through her glossy tresses. "Do you like it? I promised Jane, she has a plan... Not sure what it is exactly, but it's Jane's plan, so it will be amazing."

Dirty blonde, with hints of various lighter, brighter blonde hues through it. Reminded her a little of Tripp's.

"It's beautiful." She dumped her purse on the bar and went around to snag some lemonade. "It will contrast better with your dress. Are you wearing white?"

"Jane insisted. She says it's not for the virgin thing, but like you said, white sets off my coloring better, apparently. We handed autonomy over to our beautiful Jane; what she wants, she gets." Roxie waved the words away. "Enough about that, how did it go today? Was Ackley an asshole?"

There was a correct response. Sort of a correct response. A particular response Roxie expected. Though she didn't want to disappoint her friend, she had to be fair, honest.

"I don't know." Twisting off the bottle cap, she tossed it in the trash and considered her day as she sipped. "He seemed receptive, but was that for me or him?" She shrugged and wandered toward her friend. "I don't suppose it matters. He wants to meet again tomorrow."

"And you're okay with that?"

"I get he'll have questions. And, as Bastian put it, Ackley needs a minute to figure this out for himself."

"He'll want to check you're for real."

She dropped onto the couch. "Exactly."

"And you'd be offended except you accept you're a stranger to him."

"I'm not wholly convinced he even knew of my existence before today." After another sip, she licked her lips. "One thing he did say, communication with Trish has been... sporadic."

Keeping her wiggling toes on the edge of the table, Roxie relaxed back onto the couch next to her. She held up both hands, showing her matching nails, though that wasn't the point.

"That's Zairn's deal, not mine." Roxie gestured finality in the air. "I take nothing to do with it."

"Because you disapprove?" Huh, why hadn't she thought to ask Roxie how she felt about Trish relying so heavily on a man she'd once been intimate with? The man Roxie was currently intimate with. "Are you mad he's protecting her?"

"God, no. No one else could do it, I wouldn't trust anyone else to do it." Neither would Trish, which was how they'd ended up in their predicament. "I leave it to him because I do trust him. He doesn't need me getting in between things or questioning him."

"Funny, I've heard the opposite about you."

Roxie's head rolled on her shoulders. "Okay, so it's possible, in the past, I've been known to inject myself—" She held up a pointed index finger. "—for the greater good, you understand."

"Of course," she said on a laugh.

"But this is serious shit, it's not playing. I'm always with Zairn. I'd support him in anything and he offloads on me if he needs to, when he needs to." She was familiar with that genre of relationship dynamic. "But it's a big responsibility, holding a woman's safety, her life, in his hands. He's got it covered, he knows what's expected of him."

"You do know he probably doesn't tell you more

to protect you."

"Physically? Maybe. Except if he really thought someone would try to hurt me for the information, he'd give it to me. As for emotionally? Mentally? Spiritually..." The newly minted brunette exaggerated that last one. "In every other way? No. We don't do that. It's all cards on the table, there's nothing I wouldn't share with him." Shifting, Roxie got her shoulder into the backrest to make eye contact. "Isn't it like that with you and Breck?"

"Yes," she said on a sigh. "Which is why I'm not looking forward to our next conversation. Where's Tripp?"

"At the club. He'll be back for dinner, though I do think he wants to go out tonight. Are you up for dancing the night away?"

"Yeah, maybe. "Just then, something on the TV caught her eye. "Zairn." Sitting up straight, she pointed at the screen. "Zairn's on the TV."

"So what else is new?" Roxie crunched her abs to boost herself back up and reach between her feet for the remote control to turn up the volume. "What does my love have to say?"

Except it wasn't him talking, it was only a picture of him with a reporter or someone talking over the top of the various images as they changed.

"...with the wedding so close?"

"We have attempted to reach Ms. Kyst for comment," said another reporter they couldn't see.

Roxie looked left and right. "They didn't try very hard, did they?"

"Is your phone on?"

"I'm not even sure it's in the building."

The suite door suddenly slammed and in came Tripp at a hundred miles an hour. "What the fuck?"

That was the first thing he said, and for an

explanation, all turned to the TV.

"...news of the affair has been confirmed by our sources inside the Rouge camp."

"Unnamed sources," Roxie muttered.

"Zairn and Anjelica have been involved, intimately, for months."

Tripp exhaled a laugh. "Like how they added 'intimately' there in case anyone didn't know what 'affair' meant."

"Behind Roxie's back?" the first reporter asked. A picture of a stunning blonde jumped to the screen, not Roxie, presumably it was the other woman. "Anjelica is a beautiful woman, is Ms. Kyst worried Zairn might prefer the younger model?"

"Oh, ouch..." On a laugh, Roxie shook her head. "I'm not even thirty and already I've aged out."

"Who is she? Do you know her?" she asked when Roxie muted the TV again.

"Never seen her before in my life. Doesn't mean she's not been a part of it. I suppose, apparently, she has been behind my back."

"My phone's a fucking control tower. Know how many calls I've had?" Tripp said and tossed his phone onto the couch. "Z called too, once."

"You better be lying," Roxie said, picking it up to scroll through the call list. "I have no intention of talking to him."

"Roxie," she said, stroking her back. "You should at least give him a chance to explain."

"The call was from his phone," her friend said to Tripp. "That doesn't mean it was him. It was probably Tibbs."

"Why would you—"

"I saw Breck screwing a Laker Girl in the lobby," Roxie stated. "Two of them actually, might've been three. Right there under the chandelier." Her friend arched a brow. "Believe me?"

Her head tilted. "He would never—"

"Neither would Z and he knows I know that. Trust me, we've been through all of this before. One time they accused Astrid of sleeping with him. Can you imagine? Poor girl was mortified. It's not a huge deal, it'll die down."

"They're only interested because of the wedding," Tripp said, sitting on the perpendicular couch. "This nix us going out tonight?"

"No! We never let them win. It's what they want. That younger woman is being exploited and probably doesn't know it."

"Oh, she'll know it by the number of zeroes on her check. Want me to find out?" Tripp asked, relaxing. "Find out where she is and I'll—"

"Aww, that's very sweet of you to offer to screw the truth out of Zairn's fake mistress. I'm tearing up." Roxie blew out a long breath, fanning her face. "This is not a thing. Let's just go about our lives as normal. No one has to worry about this. There's zero truth in it."

"It doesn't piss you off that they're saying these things about the man you love?"

"Of course it pisses me off, but I've done the angry at the media thing before. Only one who ends up exhausted is me. Don't fuel their fire. I'll stream tonight. Soon as people see me making fun of the story, they'll lose their steam."

Wow, this woman was a pro.

"Okay then," Tripp said and clapped once. "What's for dinner?" His finger jumped her way. "And do not say deep dish. Some of us have a wedding to look good for. We're having a night off, pizza junkie."

"A junkie or..." When her eyes met Roxie's, the possibility glowed in them. "Could've been a false negative."

"Great." Tripp exhaled. "Just what I need, to find out I've been dragging my pregnant sister-in-law around the country, waving her in front of gangsters and assholes."

"There are gangsters and assholes in New York just the same. And I'm fine. Negative is negative."

"You can't be sure. What's with all the pizza? Feels like a craving to me."

"Which you know from the dozens of times you've been pregnant," she replied to Tripp with an incredulous, prolonged blink.

"It's not a pregnancy craving..." Her spine sprang straight. That voice came from the foyer. From in the damn room. "It's rebellion."

The moment he came into view, she jumped up and rushed to him. "Breck!"

Leaping onto him, she didn't even care that her dramatic show was over the top. Her arms locked around his neck and she buried her face there, breathing him in. It was ridiculous that her eyes watered. Why was she in such a state over him just walking in? She should be mad or uncomfortable that he'd happened upon her without invitation. Instead, joy infused her.

"What took you so long?" she mumbled against him.

He stroked from the top of her head, down her spine, and patted her ass, bending forward to put her back on her feet. On her feet, right. Yes. Polite company. Etiquette rules. At least she hadn't wrapped her legs around him and planted her mouth on his. That's what she usually did in hotel suites. Though they didn't usually have an audience. Wow, she deserved a medal for remembering there were others in the room, in the state.

Though he prompted her to take her own weight, he kept his arm tight around her, holding them together.

Tripp came over, arms open. "Good to see you,

brother."

Instead of a hug, or other warm welcome, Breck glared. "You're lucky I'm not in charge of Trust Fund Tax anymore. What have you got my girl mixed up in?"

"Hey, this one isn't me." Showing his palms in surrender, Tripp stalled. "I'm just along for the ride."

"Yeah," Breck muttered. "That's usually the way with her."

"I'm right here."

"Not for long."

"Wait…" Tripp frowned. "Does that mean Caber's in charge of Trust Fund Tax?"

TWENTY-FOUR

LINKING THEIR FINGERS, Breck took her away from the audience, without answering Tripp's question, and through to the master bedroom. Just like Bastian, he closed the door. Another talking to? What was with the men in her life? Okay, so... huh, maybe she deserved this one. Better to get a lecture and know he cared than to be ignored. Oh, it would break her heart.

"Did Bastian call?" she asked.

Was that what prompted the trip?

"No," Breck said. "But he should've."

Wandering from him, she went to sit on the edge of the bed. "I asked him not to call you. Not to tell you where I was... You knew where I was because of Roxie, right?"

He came to stand in front of her. "Were you really hiding from me?"

"No!" And she never would. "I didn't want you to feel responsible for me. I don't want you to feel responsible."

"I'm always responsible for you, and you me,

that's the way it works."

He'd been raised to believe relationships were that way. With parents who loved and adored each other as well as their children. Breck had a view of the world she'd never experienced in her own life. Not until meeting him and the Breckenridges.

"This wasn't something I wanted you involved in. I had to do this myself."

"You're at liberty to do that; I have no plans to get in the way…" Sitting at her side, he ran his fingers into her hair, catching it between them as he cradled her jaw. "If you need to do this without me, do it without me. All I want is to be waiting here for you at the end of the day. Every day."

Oh, sigh. Now he was being romantic when she could rip his clothes off. Kicking off her shoes, she slid herself back on the mattress until her legs were extended straight out.

The saucy smile wasn't really required; he'd read her mood. "I could be ovulating."

"You're not."

Damn the man and his math. "We could pretend…"

Though amusement relaxed his features, she didn't sense a ravishing was coming up next.

"You keep saying we're not doing this again." And this was the worst time to muddy the waters. He was ready for their future, and her certainty was still gray. "I won't be your sperm donor. The next time we make love, it's going to be for good, Coy. Are you ready for that? Because once we start, there's no more, 'not doing this again.' Do you understand?"

Though almost every part of her wanted to be, she hadn't started this journey only to give up before seeing it through.

Flopping from her elbows onto her back, she

pressed her foot against his thigh. "We can cuddle, can't we? Just lie together and... breathe. It's been a tough couple of days."

Her focus stayed on the ceiling though she heard him take off his shoes. Then he was scooping her up, relaxing both of them, his head in a pillow, hers on his shoulder. It did feel better to be there. Against the heat of him, the solidity, the strength. Breck could calm and agitate her atoms simultaneously and at will. As her eyes closed, she prayed he'd never stop, that this would never stop.

"Have you been sleeping?" he asked, fingers moving through her hair.

"Not as well as I do next to you." Her palm skimmed up his torso and down, checking this was real, that he really was there holding her. "I have a lot to tell you."

"You don't have to tell me anything. That's not why I came. I am not checking up on you."

"I know that. I know. I want to tell you. I always knew I'd have to, that I'd want to. The wheels are in motion now, there's nothing either of us can do to stop it. Before, I... I didn't want you to talk me out of my purpose."

"Which means you did something I'd have preferred you not do alone."

"Bastian came with me, and don't be mad at him for supporting me. I asked for his help and he did advise me, several times, to loop you in."

"I'm not mad at him for supporting you. Though I don't know how I'll ever pay him back for being with you when I couldn't." His lips grazed her hair. "Is it over? Are you finished with whatever you were doing?"

"I have a meeting tomorrow. Bastian was supposed to come with me. After I tell you everything, if you're still with me..." As in supporting her, not the other, more intimate way. "Maybe you could take Bastian's place. Though…"

Would that be a good idea? Already walking in there was risky. Did she want Breck to be seen going in there too? With her? She'd been nervous enough about Bastian and the man lived in the state, had connections in government. Maybe instead of him being with her, people would assume it was the other way around, she'd just been tagging along on one of Bastian's errands. With Breck, it wouldn't be like that. Especially when any eagle-eyed onlooker noted her going into the same office twice in the same week. Twice in as many days.

"Though what?" he asked.

She sat up, curling her legs at her side. "I'm going to tell you everything. After that, we can decide together."

"Okay." His hands relaxed on his chest. "Start talking."

And she did. Everything came out. Her intention to go to Trish, Roxie's diversion to Porter's, all the way through to Bastian leaving her at the suite door not long before Breck arrived.

"And that's it. Ackley wants to meet again tomorrow, probably wants to check out the details I gave him today, to make sure my claims are legitimate."

"Why?" he asked through narrow eyes.

Wasn't that obvious? "Because he doesn't know me and I think—"

"Why now?"

Oh, he wasn't talking about Ackley confirming whether her story held weight, Breck wanted to know why she'd begun the mission at all. Shouldn't that be obvious?

"You can't tell me that you flipped your life upside down for us and then not expect me to act. I've been clear. As long as there's a chance my father can interfere with us or exploit the connection to your family, we can't be fully committed to each other. The only way we can be together is if he's off the board completely."

"Prison. You want him behind bars." He didn't move but lingered before speaking again. "Do you want to testify?"

Why did everyone ask that? It wasn't like she'd expressed any desire to do it… ever. Okay, maybe not ever, she may have screamed it at her father once or twice as a teenager, but who didn't threaten their mafia dad with that kind of thing occasionally?

"No. I don't want to testify. I never wanted to testify."

"Because Acre and Axon can keep us safe. And if you want to go into official witness protection—"

"You'll come with me, I know," she droned. "I've already had that conversation with myself."

Sitting up, he repositioned the pillow at his back to lean against the headboard. "Now have it with me."

"I haven't been a part of my father's world for a long time. Anything I know is old news. Enter Out is still up and running, I checked. I've kept an eye on it through the years, because it was something I had that he didn't know I had."

"Your file."

And was she really surprised he knew it existed? No. He'd seen it once, lying on her dining table, during one of his first visits to her apartment. Man never forgot anything.

"I didn't know we were going to Porter, so I couldn't give him all the specifics. And Ackley, I decided it was time to play this card when I heard how intent Ackley was to get Joey. If he really is as dogged and determined as people say he is… I know that works against Roxie and Zairn. They have a legitimate conflict with him. I'm not saying I trust Ackley a million percent…"

"But while it's in his interest, there's no reason he should have conflict with you."

"He said he's having trouble communicating with Trish."

"Probably because Zairn doesn't like dealing with him, or Trish is just as pissed at Ackley for the way he treated Zairn as the rest of us."

"If I had a choice, I wouldn't—"

"You don't get to pick who's in office. Is Roxie upset with you?"

"No! She's supported me more than… she's been incredible."

"Did he ask you to testify? Ackley?"

"I think that's what he expected," she said. "When he found out who I was he… Maybe there's some moral argument here, that I should be willing to stand up in front of my father and call him out for everything."

"You're under no obligation to do anything. That said, if it's the path you choose—"

"I would never take you from your family."

"And they would never ask me to watch you walk away."

"Would you really want to raise our children that way? We'd never be safe. I wouldn't want that. I wouldn't want them to fear for their lives on a daily basis. The life we have, we could have, the one I'm fighting for, doesn't involve us running and hiding."

"We can give Porter the file."

"Yes," she said. "Although I don't know how to get it to him without using means that could be tracked."

Phone calls would be on record; the postal service and couriers would keep paperwork too. Maybe it meant another trip to Chicago in the not-too-distant future.

"I can take care of that."

Proof she wasn't on this journey alone any longer. Why had she ever thought she might be? Roxie and Tripp had been there, Bastian had been there, but Breck... he didn't just exist beside her, he was her, and just as invested in the possibilities of their future.

Slipping her hand under his, she laced their fingers together again. "This isn't a done deal, not yet. We'll have to wait, I don't know how long."

"What are we waiting for? Your father to be arrested again? A trial? Sentencing? Our life is on hold."

"Your life doesn't have to be," she said, attempting to withdraw her hand. His fingers clamped around hers, proving he wouldn't let her go anywhere. "You never have to wait. I've never asked you to wait and if you're done—"

"I'm with you now," he said. "I'm not waiting to be with you, I am with you, whether you accept that or not." That was sweet. He sure didn't make it easy for a woman to uphold her resolve. "But you want something, now, and I don't want you to wait. Not for the sake of a family who never deserved you."

"A child was a good idea..." in her head anyway, "when I thought we'd be the only ones to know its parentage. But someone..." Her eyes widened as she bowed a little his way. "Someone went around telling everyone."

He remained impervious. "Do you really think they wouldn't have known?"

"Maybe they'd have suspected, but if we'd stuck to concealing the truth..."

"I could never have lied about something like that."

"I didn't ask you to lie, just not offer anything."

"My mother would've asked."

"Like you've never tap-danced around your

mother's questioning before."

"Do you think she would be a bad grandparent? A negative influence?"

"No." This time she did take her hand away, regardless of his fight to keep it. "I love your family, but I can't keep them safe, not while my father is free to walk the streets."

"They can keep you safe—"

"No, God…" Climbing off the bed, she took a few breaths before stopping at the bottom. "We've had this argument."

"I don't want your needs to be on hold, to leave the future up to strangers."

"Yes, I want to have children. That is my need. But it's also my need that they live safely. That's the priority, the safety of our children."

Something she couldn't yet promise him.

"Okay," he said on an exhale. "I'll do it your way."

He always did. In the end.

Good.

Now maybe they could forget their stresses for a minute.

"Are you going to take me out to dinner now?" she asked, ready to move on from the topic of her father.

"If you're paying…"

"Oh, that's right," she teased. "You've taken a vow of poverty."

"It's not a vow."

"But, wait, how did you get here if…"

Her suspicion didn't come to fruition; his next words gave her the answer.

"We've been invited to Carolyn's for dinner."

"Ca—Bastian's mom? How does she know you're in town?" Her lips quirked until her cheeks bulged. "Your momma brought you here, didn't she?"

Carolyn Hunt and Alice Breckenridge had been friends all their lives. They'd grown up together. "Aww, that's so sweet."

"She was coming to LA this month anyway."

"Aww," she mocked in her swoon. "That's adorable. Your mommy gave you a ride."

"Mm hmm," he said, not amused, but not riled either. He got up off the bed. "Tripp and Roxie are invited too."

"They want to go to the club. Maybe they'll come to eat, but they've done so much for me. They should have a night off."

"They can have the rest of the trip off now I'm here," he said, sliding his hands onto her waist. "We may as well stay."

"I have to get a dress for the wedding."

"Mom will help you out with that."

"I can afford my own dress," she said, unable to hide her smile. "Do you need me to get you a tux too? We should discuss an allowance if you're expecting me to support you financially. You know, a little bit of freedom money, so your masculinity isn't threatened by coming to me hat in hand."

"I meant…" he said, pacing his words and his breathing. "Mom can help with the traipsing around stores, trying on fifty different things only to end up back where you started."

"Why palm me off on your mom?" she asked, pressing herself close. "It's not like you have anything else to do."

"This is a good time for me to look around. Maybe I'll get a job in LA."

"We are not LA people," she said, stroking him. "And I do not want to raise LA children."

"My mom was raised in California."

"Yes, and now she lives in New York. Where we

live." Stating it categorically was as much playing as it was sincere. "We will have New York children—if we have them."

"That will be fun."

"I have to take a shower before we go out. Will you talk to Tripp and Roxie? Find out their plans?"

"Yes. Then I'll come and check you're okay."

"Oh no," she said, slinking out of his arms, wiggling a finger his way. "You had your chance, buddy. If you wanted to see the good stuff, you should've taken advantage of my surprise you were here, when I was all soft and gooey and grateful."

"You'll give in one day."

"One day."

One day, she would. Hell, she'd have him right there in the moment if it wouldn't mean disappointing him again. Being intimate with him was her greatest pleasure. Reminding him that the shackles of commitment remained loose, that was her biggest sadness. He was ready. She had to hurry the hell up.

TWENTY-FIVE

NO DOUBT BRECK forewarned the mothers not to ask questions at dinner. Though it may not have been necessary. Alice and Carolyn were savvy parents used to their children leading their own lives their own ways. More so the latter than the former. In honesty, the whole prying thing sort of didn't apply to them anyway. With all the ups and downs of her and Breck's relationship, whatever the answer in the morning, it wasn't always the same in the evening, so why waste the breath?

Roxie and Tripp tagged along for the evening meal, but, as suspected, slunk off to the club later while she and Breck went back to the hotel suite alone. And before anyone asked, yes, they slept together, no, they didn't have sex. That surprise deserved a high five... and possibly a cold shower. As much as she wanted him, disappointing him overrode her selfish desire. Giving in would only be cruel. She couldn't make any promises and didn't want to give him false hope. This could still all go to shit.

While their friends still slumbered, she and Breck

had breakfast in bed, checked out the news, and discussed the media furor around Zairn's "affair."

"Roxie was completely unaffected. It just bounced right off like they were talking about a stranger," she said, forcing herself to put the coffee back on the provided over-bed table. The Grand was full service; every eventuality was accounted for. "I should shower, my meeting's in an hour."

"Our meeting," Breck said, folding his newspaper to put it on the table too.

Always efficient, he'd already showered. He did that while she lounged in bed waiting for their breakfast to appear.

"I'm still not convinced you should come. People shouldn't see us together."

"You have never cared about being seen with me in New York. Or anywhere else. We've been seen on the streets of LA together before."

"We've never been seen together entering a District Attorney's office. This could be dangerous."

"Which is not a recommended argument when trying to convince me it's better you do this alone." In only his underwear, he got out of the bed to rise to full-height and hubba-hubba, why hadn't she taken advantage of him the previous night? "I'll call and change the appointment."

Didn't that just shake loose the abs distraction. "Change it? Why would you—I don't want to change it. How long do you expect us to be in LA? I won't take advantage of your father's kindness indefinitely. First, he loses you, then you drag his wife across the country because of me."

"Breckenridge will survive without us."

"I don't want it to survive without us, I want it to survive with us, to need us."

"Okay," he said, and came to rest his hands on

her shoulders without doing a great job of hiding how he enjoyed her being overwrought. "Calm down. I wasn't suggesting we should delay the meeting. We'll change the location. Have him come here."

His logic made sense in the face of her argument but... "Are you sure that's a great idea with Roxie—she's paying for the suite and—"

"It's Bastian's hotel, no one is paying for anything."

That wasn't the soundest business model, probably why she always forgot it. They didn't pay for things because the families went way back. As for Roxie, she probably paid in the past, before her introduction to Bastian. Though... Zairn knew him, so maybe she hadn't. Did anyone pay for anything? How did these billionaires make money or stay rich when they gave so much away?

"Still wouldn't be polite to bring Ackley into her personal space."

"We can do it downstairs, in another room or suite. Or I'll talk to Roxanna and—"

"Why doesn't she like Bastian?"

"Why doesn't she—I have no idea. What makes you think she doesn't like him?"

"I think she's okay with him now, but when we introduced them she seemed, I don't know... wary. I'm curious."

"Ask Tripp."

Yeah, that would be a better idea except they hadn't been alone long enough for it to come up. It couldn't be like she was too eager to pry.

But while on the subject of unknown information... "You didn't tell me Bastian and Robyn split up."

"Does it upset you? You were never fond of her."

"She didn't care about Bastian. They were together but, she was cold, Bastian deserves better than cold; he's not cold. And there was no equality, it was always him running around after her."

"Darroch runs around after Savanna, you have no objection to her. None you've voiced to me."

Her head dropped to the side. "You only have to look at them together to know she's as besotted by him as he is by her. You notice it more from the guy side because he's your brother."

"She needed a lot of coaxing to accept the lifestyle. Still does."

"And she loves your brother in spite of that."

Breck's brows rose. "In spite of him being rich? It's hardly a failing."

"Money doesn't excuse all sins. Not everyone is comfortable with it. Roxie wasn't, sometimes still isn't, she just hides it better."

"It will be interesting to see how that plays out at the wedding."

"Because it will be a big, grand show? No expense spared? That's for the people, the fans, not for her. Her best friend, Jane, organized the whole thing because she likes that sort of thing. Weddings and bows, and... the pretty, fluffy things. I think if it was down to Roxie and Zairn themselves, they'd have eloped."

"Not easy to elope when you have such recognizable faces."

"There's something romantic about it, isn't there?" she asked, skimming her arms around him to hold herself close. Of course that meant her head went back and the slow moistening of his lips betrayed how he liked lording over the view. "They're so well known, the world think they know them, but they still hold something of themselves back."

"Is that what you want now? Fame?"

"Good God, no." Which he knew. "We're not that different to them, if you think about it. Everyone knows we're together, they just don't... know."

"They don't understand."

"Yes."

"Coy, baby, sometimes I don't understand."

On a laugh, she buried her face against his chest. "Isn't that what makes the chase so fun?"

"For the first five years, maybe. Now I wonder if you'll ever stop running."

The air crackled. "I don't want to make promises I can't keep. Whichever way it goes, the finish line is in sight, I promise, Stat. I promise. One way or the other—"

"That's what you don't understand. You think there's a choice in this for me."

"There is."

"You are my choice, Sequoia, and whatever the hell shit we have to deal with—"

"Don't swear." Her arms dropped as she stepped away. "You know how to express yourself better than that."

He should given the price of his education.

"You don't realize how much of your past you carry around every minute."

Not smart to remind her. "If I'm so burdened, why put up with me at all?"

"That's what I'm trying to explain. I've accepted it. I accepted it long ago. I love you for it. God, I know you better than you know yourself."

She couldn't deny he had an astounding way of anticipating her, but that statement was a helluva presumptive.

"If you knew me that well, you'd know this isn't a choice for me either. We will be together if my father is out of the way—"

"Your father lives in your head, Coy. He always has. I know that part of you, accept that part of you, love that part of you."

"You love me for being screwed up by my father?"

"I love that in spite of your start, you've made an incredible life for yourself. Why can't you let me be a part of it?"

"Because I love you, and I don't want to ruin you."

"You know what some of my brothers have been through." When she tried to turn away, he grabbed her shoulder to bring her back. "What my family has been through with them. Do we ever turn them away and say it's too hard?"

"That's what you do for family. You fight for them."

Virtuous family anyway, the exact opposite of hers.

"You are my family. Name or not, you've been a Breckenridge since before we ever met. You've been a Breckenridge since before you met any of us. It happened the moment my father got the call from yours. He'd never let anyone live like that, with the constrictions, the chains, the dictatorship. The disrespect. Whether you worked for the company or not, he'd have made sure you were one of us."

"Oh, so it was my sob story that got me the job? All these years I've worked for the company and you're telling me it's nothing to do with my ability, and everything to do with my oppression? Thanks. I wish one of you let that slip out sooner."

"Nothing slips out of me. My words are always deliberate." His grip on her shoulder tightened to pull her back. "My father adores you, my mother, my brothers, all of us. We want you to be a part of our family and you keep pushing us away."

"For your own good."

"And now we're going to have a child—"

"I'm not pregnant."

"Whether you're carrying my child this instant or not is irrelevant, it's going to happen." And with his steely determination focused solely on her, she couldn't refute that. No matter how many times they tried to end it, the line beneath their sexual relationship always grayed. "Roxie was right, we should get another test."

"The pizza thing—"

"Is no coincidence. Your father's looming large in our lives again and you start breaking his rules."

What was he...? "No pizza," she whispered.

"No junk food. Wasn't Joey allowed to eat and drink anything he wanted? His girls weren't allowed to make poor food choices, to gain weight, to be 'sloppy' as he called it." Maybe she shouldn't have been so open with Breck through the years. "Some part of your subconscious wants to remind you that you're an adult, disconnected from that previous life, capable of making your own decisions."

A few seconds of reflection stretched. It took her mind a while to catch up with his words.

"Decisions you don't accept. I am making my own decisions; they're just not the ones you want me to make."

"You want a child. Isn't having a baby your decision? I want to make that happen. We agree on—"

"We agreed before you went around telling everyone. Now I'm not sure it can ever happen."

Because even if she went to a sperm bank, no one would ever believe any of her offspring weren't Breck's. And her promise to him... it wasn't even about her promise, her biology rebelled against the idea of carrying another man's child. The idea physically sickened her. Which was crazy because not all the Breckenridges were blood.

Having Breck's child was an exciting notion. It thrilled her. A zing of desperate excitement shot through her every time the idea seeded itself. There was a future she wanted, he was right. Except aspiring to something didn't change the circumstances.

"I won't leave you wanting."

No, he never did. Why couldn't he see she valued him just the same?

"You deserve so much happiness. This life— what I put you through. It's unfair. Can't you see how much simpler your life would be if you just... let go..."

"All these years..." His hand fell to his side as the corner of his mouth curled. "It's never occurred to me once."

The back of his fingers drifted across her cheek and she moistened her lips in anticipation of his. Had she ever convinced herself she wasn't his wholly and completely? Where was the line now?

The sudden blare of the phone by the bed startled them both; he hid it better. Leaving her there without his kiss, frustrated, and a little petulant, he went to answer it.

TWENTY-SIX

SHOWER. YES. That's where she'd been headed. Breck would deal with whoever was on the phone and didn't need supervision. She slipped into the bathroom before he could finish the call. If she delayed to satisfy her curiosity about the identity of the interrupter, they'd only get sucked into another discussion and, as she'd said, time was running short.

The routine of washing and preparing herself for the day gave a focus. Any time she considered what Ackley may say, what he'd found out, what he wanted from her to continue on, she redoubled her effort to exfoliate or moisturize or whatever else she was doing. Dwelling wouldn't change the outcome.

Drying her hair was a quick affair. She went with just a little makeup, enough that the effort would be noticed, not far enough that it looked like impressing anyone was on her agenda. At least with Breck at her side, she wouldn't have to contend with any leering. Ackley wasn't the overt sort, as such, he just carried an air most women would recognize as creepy. Breck wouldn't stand for it if any man tried anything with her, and it wasn't jealousy, he hated the disrespect. All Breckenridges were big on that.

Clothes took a little longer than usual. The closet was full and nothing was hers. Each time she settled on something, another something would catch her eye. Nothing wrong with researching the options.

Though, shit, time, time, time. Finishing up, she hurried through to the living room expecting Breck, Roxie, maybe even Tripp. She didn't expect to see Breck enjoying coffee with Alice and Carolyn.

"Good morning," Alice said, bright and beautiful, as always.

"Is it still morning?" she asked and went to bend down to pour coffee into one of the clean cups. "Roxie and Tripp are still asleep."

"I told them that," Breck said. "And that we have an appointment downstairs."

She straightened up. "You changed it?"

"The man we're meeting did," he said. "I'm not sure of the specific developments."

Something must've changed for Ackley to avoid his office. What would it be...? There was that speculation again, and she had no soaps or shampoos to distract her.

"All very cloak and dagger," Carolyn said.

"Not really," she said, though that wasn't far off. "It's just…complicated, and really not that interesting."

Yes, she could feel Breck mentally poking her. Okay, so it may impact whether one of the present parties became a grandparent, but was that necessary to talk about now?

"We didn't come to interrupt your day." Alice sipped her coffee. "With the wedding nearing, we just wanted to be of help."

"Roxie's who you have to talk to about that," she

said. "And Rox might direct you to Jane. I imagine everything is in hand." Did that sound defensive? She didn't mean it to and adored both women. "Though I'm sure she'd love the help."

"Jane went back to New York to help Lilya with the baby," Alice said and glowed when she smiled. "She can't stay away and I don't blame her. The little one is perfect. Have you met him?"

"The baby?" She shook her head. "No. I've heard he's adorable though."

Had she? When Roxie talked about him. He was a little prince, one who'd want for nothing, born into love, hope, and prosperity. He had an incredible future ahead of him, filled with nothing but possibility. His parents wouldn't dictate who he could build a life with because he wouldn't have to worry about protecting their wellbeing.

"You'll meet him at the wedding."

A little, squishy baby, maybe a month old... Now she wasn't sure if Breck was the one prodding her heart or if that came from the need of her ovaries.

"Breck says you need a dress." Alice put her cup down. "For the wedding."

Mm, of course he had.

"Unfortunately, my appointment has to take precedence over wardrobe."

"Oh, we understand. There's a superb stylist in town," Carolyn said, phone already in hand. "She'll bring everything here, and you can try it on this evening."

"I..." This time she did let her attention track to Breck. "I might not be here tonight."

"Plans? If it's the nightclub—"

"She's worried about Dad falling apart without her." Breck: the squealer. "The company crumbling and foundering without her input."

"I didn't say that—" she said to him, then turned

it on the mothers. "I didn't say that."

Alice was amused, not offended. "Don't you worry about Ben or the company."

"I'm not—I love my job."

"It's a tough time to slack, given she's looking for a promotion," Breck said, earning himself another demerit. "I don't work for the company anymore, babe. It's out of my hands."

That wouldn't be the only thing far from his hands any time soon. Her decision to abstain in bed last night was all the brighter. Hope he wasn't holding his breath for later.

"I'm happy with the job I have," she said. "And I'd like to keep it."

Alice and Carolyn laughed at the same time. Beyond besties, they were more like sisters.

"Ben would never take away your job," Alice said.

Highly amusing, maybe, not so much after her conversation with Breck.

"One day Ben's job will belong to your children." And there was Carolyn's bold tenacity. "Never forget that. I doubt he does."

She'd skate on by that landmine.

"I don't know." Her revelation would shift the gears. "I did find out I only got my job because I was pathetic and Ben pitied me. That was fun news. No chance of a promotion for that person, is there?"

Not so quick to open his mouth, Breck found his reliable glare. The women weren't laughing anymore.

"That's not true," Alice said, sort of devastated, which hadn't been her intention. "Breck, did you tell Sequoia—"

"I didn't say that." His firm tone was more boardroom than bedroom, but if he wanted to speak up, so be it. "She's a Breckenridge. I told her that happened, her inclusion in our family, before we met. That Dad would never have tolerated what Coy's father put her through. My falling in love with her was incidental; she's a Breckenridge with or without my affection."

"Now that is true."

Did he have to bring up her father like that? Her whole "complicated" explanation put that to bed, didn't it? She didn't want the pus from her tormented mental wounds to rain on anyone.

"Is your father in LA?" Carolyn asked.

Oh, great, so that mention hadn't dashed by unnoticed. Had he honestly expected it would? This was the number one subject she wanted to avoid.

"I hope not, I don't speak with him or follow his calendar." Now she sounded defensive again. "It's a complicated situation."

Carolyn knew who she was, who she really was, without her mother's maiden name. They'd been a part of each other's lives sporadically, more so at family events or social situations when she was with Breck. As for sitting down and pouring it all out, yeah, she didn't have the energy for that. Or time! Time, time, time.

"We're going to be late, Stat," she said, tapping at an invisible watch. "If you want to stay here with your mom—"

"No." Breck stood, straightening his slacks and his cuffs. Jeans and a tee-shirt would have been inappropriate, yes. Was it any more appropriate that he was wearing a tie? Showed the rest of them up. The "rest of them" being her. "Given you don't know where the meeting is, since our change of venue, I think it's important I tag along."

Hmm, yeah, match point.

"Do you have to wear a tie?" she asked, wrapping her fingers around it when he reached her side. "You do the whole sexy bossman thing, I'll forget our purpose."

His mom was in the room. Did that matter? Throughout the duration of their relationship, Alice Breckenridge had seen, and heard, her do or say much worse with her son.

"Yes, I have to wear a tie. You didn't drink your coffee."

Observant, wasn't he?

"I got enough coffee this morning."

Okay and the way she'd said that made it seem like she wasn't talking about java. Something about him being close to her melted her bones. She was maybe supposed to be mad at him... why was that again?

He looked to his mother. "Do you want me to wake Tripp before I leave?"

Good question. Better Breck go in there and find whatever carnage Tripp brought back from the club last night, than his mother witness any horrors. Plus, Tripp slept naked, and no relative wanted to see that. The woman might have changed his diapers, but he'd changed a whole lot since then... she'd suppose, and didn't want to imagine. When the choice was him or his mother, Breck would take one for the team. Tripp would probably prefer his brother do the waking too. All the Breckenridge men adored Alice, few other women got a second look when it came to their maternal dedication.

"No, I'll just—"

"Mr. Breckenridge?"

Their butler's voice brought them all around. Usually when someone addressed that name, there was a cornucopia of people available to answer to it. This time, there was only one.

Breck stepped up. "Is there a problem?"

"You have a guest," the butler said.

Another one? What the hell? Had they brought Times Square with them? Their unplanned trip was supposed to be discreet. You know, secret, unknown.

They'd been failing on that from before they even touched down. She wasn't used to being so popular. Except, hmm, okay, maybe Breck was the exception; he didn't really count as a guest.

"Bring them in." Breck's impatience was appreciated. Maybe now he was getting her persistence about the hour. "We don't have a lot of time."

As the butler retreated, she spun around to Breck. "We don't have time at all."

"The meeting is in the building, Coy, relax. There's no travel time." He stroked her cheek. "And they want this as much as we do. No one's walking away."

It was supposed to set their relationship free; the fact Ackley and his cohorts would relish the win was a bonus. But Breck was right, that did keep the power balance teetering. Except, who cared? This wasn't business. She didn't care who blinked first or who had more power. This wasn't a negotiation that ended with zeroes on a check, this was so much more important. Of all people, Breck should understand that.

"And I thought our Grand Hotel was fancy…"

Her jaw relaxed as back she went and… "Porter." She couldn't believe it. Couldn't explain it. Didn't even have a guess as to… "What are you doing here?"

"You tell me, Ms. Gambatto. What am I doing here?"

TWENTY-SEVEN

HOW DID SHE explain this? The polite thing to do would be to introduce Porter, except... Who was he? She couldn't go into detail. The fewer people who knew her connection to Porter, the better. If she went the other way... dropping Roxie in it wouldn't be fair. So who was, Porter, their surprise guest, supposed to be exactly...?

"Uh..."

"Mom—"

"What a thing to wake up to..." Roxie's voice cut Breck's off and got everyone's attention. "I've told you, Porter, how many times, you have to get over me. We're over. You're poor. Move on..."

That could be meant as a joke... or not. Breck had stepped in valiantly, which was a testament to his honor because, as far as she knew, the two men had never met. His attempts to introduce Porter would be more strained than hers.

Roxie had joined them at exactly the right moment. In a man's shirt, legs bare, the brunette scooped up her tousled hair to toss it down her back.

"RoRo—"

"Do we need to have another conversation?" Roxie marched on over to grab Porter's cuff. He wasn't wearing a tie. If Porter didn't need a tie, why did Breck? "Come with me and don't say another word."

Good. Roxie saved the day. And that was a stretch of friendship. The beauty dragged Porter back the way she'd come and, presumably, into her bedroom. Not somewhere an affianced woman should be taking an ex-boyfriend only a day after the groom-to-be was accused of having his own affair.

"Oh, that poor man," Carolyn said like she was buying it. "He must love her dearly."

"Not easy for any man to compete with Zairn Lomond."

Was Alice duped too? It didn't feel nice to misdirect such a kind and generous woman.

Her eyes met Breck's.

"I should go and check they're okay."

Her feet were already taking her backwards. Breck didn't say anything; what could he say? What she wanted him to do was get rid of the matriarchs. How exactly could she request he do that without offending them or tantalizing suspicions?

Backwards, backwards. At the last second, she spun to hurry into the hallway to Roxie's bedroom.

"...crazy person showing up here..." Roxie's voice snapped her trajectory to the closet. "What did you think that was going to achieve?"

"I was told to come here."

Porter was just inside the closet while Roxie was further inside dragging a comb through her lush hair.

"Who told you to come here, Porter?" Sequoia asked, incidentally announcing her presence with the question. "Do you mean to California or specifically up to the suite? You can't do that, show up where I am.

People don't know we know each other. Haven't you ever heard of discretion? It's something a man in your profession should understand."

Roxie waved the comb in agreement. "See, listen to the woman, that's what I said."

"Even if you didn't care about blowing my cover, what about Roxie?" she asked Porter. "Did you even consider what Zairn would think?"

The comb dropped to Roxie's side. "Zairn? Why would he care?"

"We used to sleep together, you know," Porter said like Roxie had to be reminded. The brunette's expression morphed to enjoyment, no concern for miles. "I think she's implying this rendezvous could be a rekindling of the flame, RoRo."

"You think he might be threatened by you? By any man? Have you met Zairn Lomond? My Casanova?"

"The guy was accused of having his own affair yesterday."

Turning around, Roxie propped herself against the vanity. "So you think maybe you saw your chance and showed up to win me back? Oh, or that I called you to come here and get revenge?" Roxie perked up so bright, she bounced on her tiptoes. "Oh my God, that's what the press will think... How exciting!" Looking this way and that, the woman didn't find whatever she sought. "We're in LA, we need Crosby. Where's Tripp's cellphone?"

"With Tripp, probably," Porter said. "And I already talked to Zairn. He's the only guy I know still working at that time like it's four in the afternoon. Do you think I was getting on a plane without checking this was for real? Don't get many calls at four a.m. demanding I get my ass on a plane to LA. I wasn't going anywhere without verification."

"Instead of calling me, the woman you used to

screw, you called my lover?"

"Says the woman attempting to steal other men's cellphones. How was I supposed to get in touch with the woman I used to screw when she doesn't have a working number?"

Good point. "Borrowing other men's cellphones. *Borrowing*," Roxie insisted. "I can't believe my Casanova chose now to be all about discretion. We talked like ten minutes ago; he didn't tell me you'd be showing up."

"Surprise!" he sold it deadpan. "But I'm not here to see you, RoRo."

"Why are you here?" she asked because the fundamental reason was important. "How did you know where we were?"

"Well, for starters, everyone knows where RoRo is because she's a fricking media tornado wherever she goes."

With the comb back in her hair, Roxie checked Porter's reflection in the mirror. "Jealous? I could be a congressperson right now, if it wasn't for the whole politics thing… I have presence. Appeal. I'm a popular woman."

"So popular your ex couldn't keep away."

"It's an excellent reason for him to be here in LA," Roxie said. "This will play so well. It's exactly the hype we need before the wedding. To remind everyone, you know, how glamorous and torrid our lives are."

"My life's just fine without torrid and glamorous, thanks," Porter said. "I'm so damn happy you're on another man's plate, I'll happily walk you down the aisle with your father and pay Zairn to take you off our hands."

"Ha-ha," Roxie drolled and tossed the comb to the counter. "Ah!" An apparent epiphany. "Tripp's phone is in my bed."

With purpose, Roxie marched between both of them to return to the bedroom and search the covers for a phone.

"Why is his phone in your bed?"

"How else was I going to talk to Zairn?"

"Yeah, shocking anyone might consider you have your own means of communication."

"I do have my own, though I don't know where it is. I have a lot of them. Astrid has the original… I think, maybe."

"And Astrid is…?"

"In New York," Roxie said, dialing the phone. "Now, shh, I need to have a private conversation. You two should figure this out."

Roxie went back into the closet and closed the door. A few seconds later, the shower went on in the bathroom beyond. Maybe Tripp would be minus his own phone soon. Minus as in the thing would get waterlogged, when it came to ownership, he'd already lost that. For now anyway.

In the ensuing calm, she reoriented herself to focus on the Chicago ADA.

"You got a call?" she asked. "At four a.m.?" It didn't make sense. "Who called you at four in the morning?"

What could be so urgent that they couldn't wait for business hours? Or even semi-respectable hours?

"My boss."

"The State's Attorney? Why would a Chicago—"

"Because there's a case here. Something hot that needs to be nailed down. Orders from the top."

She didn't follow. "The top?"

"Ackley," Breck said, flipping her around on the spot. Where had he come from? Her guy was more interested in the ADA beyond than her. "He wants you in this meeting."

"Porter Clement, meet—"

"Rankin Breckenridge," the prosecutor interrupted and was already striding on by her, hand outstretched to Breck. "I know who you are, sir." He got a sir? "Was that your mother I saw—"

"Yes, and she knows nothing about the situation." Breck's stern air wasn't one to be messed with. See when he did that, and with the tie... Yum. He wasn't playing fair. "Sequoia trusted you and you almost compromised her."

"It wasn't my intention. I believed Sequoia knew what was going on."

"What is going on?"

"I don't know. I have no details."

When Breck's eyes met hers, she heard his silent request. Yes, he was still doing angry eyes, and he was happy to be the bad guy, if necessary. Such a strong man with means far beyond hers, in every way, not only financial, and he was asking for direction. That was how much she mattered to him. Whatever light she had, it would always reinforce his.

"We have a meeting downstairs with Ackley," she said, gaze still on Breck's. "If Ackley wants Porter in this meeting, he must've found something..."

"Related to Chicago," Porter said. "My boss did tell me to act with absolute authority."

"Suggesting Ackley's interested in giving you something."

"What could he have?" she asked, going just an inch closer. "Something he didn't have yesterday? Something he didn't have when we met with him."

"Not necessarily," Breck said, still disregarding Porter. The guy's hand was at his side again, having never been graced by Breck's. "Maybe he didn't want to trust you until he could be sure he could trust you."

So Ackley withheld something? That wouldn't do much to ingratiate him or encourage her to further loosen her tongue.

"If LA can help Chicago prosecute my father, I support that," she said, edging toward a decision. "But I don't like men acting in concert, excluding the only woman—"

"I don't think it was meant that way."

"Don't talk over her," Breck said, maintaining his intimidating air. "You want to prove you respect her, then show her respect."

Porter blanched, his hairline retreated as his Adam's apple bobbed. "I apologize, I didn't mean to… I have great respect for Sequoia. I have great respect for you."

"Breck understands the seriousness of the situation." Playing almost mediator, she didn't mind having a defender in her corner. One much stauncher than Bastian; one who had no boundaries when it came to shielding her. "He understands why I value the outcome so much. It's extremely important to both of us. Perhaps if you tell us more about your conversation this morning…"

"It's not completely unheard of for me to get a call late at night. If there's been an incident and they need a prosector on-scene, I might get a call."

"How often does that call come from State's Attorney Unst?"

"Never." Porter's head swung left and right, sending a clear signal he wanted to give them equal attention. "That call never comes from the SA."

"So you knew something was different as soon as you picked up?"

"As soon as I got with it. Until about halfway through the conversation, I thought it was a dream. That I imagined the whole thing."

"What did he say?" Breck asked.

"He told me to get my ass on a plane to LA. That I shouldn't wait until daybreak, I had to move fast." Why the urgency? "I wasn't going to question him. All I asked was what I should do when I got here."

"And he said?"

"Go to the Platinum Suite of the Grand Hotel. That I was needed in a meeting."

"You didn't think to ask more than that?"

"I asked what it was in relation to, though I did have my suspicions. He said it was related to the case, that I'd find out more when I got here."

"Did you know what case?"

"The only case I'm working right now is your father's. Tim's doing his part, but this is the most important case either of us has on the docket. This is..."

"I know how earth-shattering it is," she said, refraining from rolling her eyes. Just. "It's career defining. Ground-breaking. News-making. Headline-grabbing..."

"I don't mean to imply your father deserves any kind of reverence. What he's done... You made it clear how important it is for him to be stopped, and I want to make that happen for you, for all of Chicago. Taking your brother off the streets is one thing, that's cutting off the tail."

"Without taking the head, you'll never kill the beast."

"No," Porter answered Breck. "We will not." If only they could have certainty that would happen. "Is DA Ackley coming here?"

Wouldn't that be great, Alice, Carolyn, some Hollywood stylist with racks of clothes and accessories, and them, waiting for Ackley to show up and blast them all to hell. What if Ackley didn't summon Porter because of her father? Maybe it was Joey. Maybe it was her. What had she ever done that LA's DA might think to summon another prosecutor? It couldn't be anything... this wasn't a gang against her... Yet, somehow, she didn't feel like this bolstered her team either.

Porter had been fine with her, great; they'd made good ground working together. In Chicago. Hmm, yeah, in Chicago. That felt an awful distance, in time and space, from their suite in LA. What might've changed since then?

"Do you have experience with DA Ackley?" she asked.

"We had one conversation, over the telephone."

"Today?"

"No, months ago. Before I knew about Joey, before Trish agreed to testify."

Curious. "Why did you call him?"

"I didn't. He called me."

"To...?"

"Tell me..." And the movement of his shoulders returned him to the awkward squirming of a few moments ago. "About Zairn's involvement in Dayah's death. His alleged involvement."

"Which is false," Breck was quick to add. "Zairn Lomond had nothing to do with Dayah Lynn's death."

"I'm aware of that now."

"You weren't then?"

"I didn't know Zairn then, we'd never met. Roxie came to me after my conversation with Ackley about Dayah. Told me Zairn had nothing to do with it."

"And you believed her?"

"I believed it after Zairn brought Trish to me and Tim. That was a long night."

"You didn't trust a woman you once loved?" she asked, the notion foreign to her. "You can't have loved her very much."

Porter shook his head. "It was a different time.

Zairn and I were strangers. Roxie's relationship with him was still… They weren't public, but I could see she was infatuated with him."

"You trusted the woman, but not her feelings."

Was Breck aiming at her? "You better trust me and my feelings."

"Sometimes with you I don't know, Coy."

Okay, the deadpan thing was funny when everyone in the room got it. Porter didn't know Breck that well.

"Truth be told," Porter said. "I was worried about her. Roxie. She's usually got her head screwed on, doesn't take any shit. With Zairn, I could tell it was different just from the way she talked about him. I didn't want her to be taken in, I wanted to protect her."

"From a potential murderer." Breck got there before she did. "I can understand that."

Okay, were they bonding now? This was no time for bromance.

"We have a meeting to get to," she said because they had to be overdue for Ackley. "The only way we find out what is going on, is to get there and hear it from him. So can we…?"

Another tap of her non-existent watch.

"Yes," Breck said, raising an arm, which she went to immediately, allowing his hand to settle on the small of her back. "We shouldn't keep him waiting any longer."

"Is Roxie coming to the meeting?" Porter asked.

Breck paused. "Do we need her?"

"The woman is getting married soon." And had already done so much for them. "She doesn't need this kind of pressure right now. Plus…"

"Ackley isn't a fan." Breck voiced what she hadn't wanted to verbalize. "We don't want the meeting to be antagonistic."

And that meant everyone had to keep their egos

in check. At the last meeting, Bastian, at least, didn't have skin in the game, both Breck and Porter did.

Without hesitation, Porter nodded. "I'll follow your lead."

What did that mean? He'd walk away if Breck told him to walk away? She doubted that. This was "career-defining," remember? If Porter Clement had to stand up to someone, would it be someone as powerful as LA DA Ackley? Instinct said no... she could be alone, out on a limb, no allies, and the potential for her father to learn what she'd done. And that was kind of terrifying...

Or it was until the press of a hand on her back guided her from the room. As powerful as LA DA Ackley? How about as powerful as Rankin "Breck" Breckenridge? Her guy may not put criminals behind bars, but when it came to getting a man elected... or not... She'd put money on her guy coming out on top every time.

TWENTY-EIGHT

THE CONFERENCE ROOM table only had six seats around it. Not a huge room, but a quiet one in a less-frequented corner of the business suite. Good start. Ackley was there with an aid who shuffled out and closed the door only moments after she, Breck, and Porter arrived.

"We have a lot to talk about," Ackley said, opening his hands to the empty seats as he descended into his own. "I thought it best this happen without too many spectators."

Was that why he moved the meeting from his office to the hotel? His discretion was intriguing. Either he was eager for further cooperation and wanted it to look like he gave a crap about her safety, or he himself had something to hide.

"What exactly is this?" With Breck seated at one side and Porter on the other, it may look like they were mob-handed, but Porter owed them nothing. "Why do we need a Chicago ADA so urgently?"

"I checked out what you told me yesterday."

Nice of Ackley to only focus on her. A show of respect or was he afraid to address either man? She'd reserve judgment. "Spoke to some people, checked out a few things."

And she wouldn't be offended by the implication of a lack of trust. Fair was fair.

"I won't ask how that turned out because I know my information is solid. You won't intimidate me."

"That's not my intention. One of the names you gave me... an associate of your father's." Yes? "An Enter Out partner confirmed what you told me."

That slammed on the mental brakes. A partner? Checking out information, fine, she expected that. Checking something out didn't include going to an accused and laying out the crime. Shouldn't business records come first? Confirm who's at the top, their income, annual statements, trace the source of the money. But talking? What was he thinking?

So much for discreet. If she had to choose one over the other, she'd rather have this meeting in the lobby than learn Ackley stomped in with undignified feet and opened his mouth to one of her father's allies.

"You spoke to..." Were such extremes so urgent? No. She'd believed—wrongly, it turned out— that he'd understand not to tip their hand to the opposition. "How could you be so...?" Oh, she wanted to scream. "He'll warn my father. Now he'll know what we're doing."

It was over before it even started. They had no chance now, her father would be covering his tracks, he had contingencies in place for this scenario. As they spoke, the water-tight doors would be slamming on every avenue of her escape.

The confidence bleeding from Ackley clenched her teeth. "He won't because that associate has agreed to testify."

Another U-turn. No. Flabbergasted, it wasn't... how was...? How was that possible?

"He what? Why would he..." And then it hit her. "For immunity. You gave him a deal."

This happened fast. Too fast? Was there such a thing? This was good. Providing said associate was for real, he'd be closer to her father, even closer than Trish. On business matters for sure. This was more than hope, it was... optimism in a cap and gown ready for the real world.

"He's a reasonable man and we have history," Ackley said. "He can be trusted."

"To look out for his own interests," Breck said, his tone conveying he wasn't convinced. "This should've been discussed before it was actioned."

"I decide how I do my job," Ackley said. "I don't need permission or guidance."

"Clearly you do, or you wouldn't be in your current position. Anything you think about doing that has the potential to get Sequoia hurt should be sanctioned before any action is taken."

"Sequoia has made it clear that she won't aid in the conviction."

Ah, so she had served her purpose and was no longer relevant?

"That doesn't make her superfluous. What she's doing is righteous and if I believe for one second you've endangered her, you won't only be run out of the state, you'll never work anywhere again. Her safety equals your continued existence."

That was vicious... and hot as hell. Her hand slipped under the table and onto his thigh. He might take it as a sign of resistance, that she didn't support what he was saying. No, he wouldn't think that. If she wanted him to stop, she'd say it. Wasn't like she'd never shown him gratitude before. Maybe they should put the sensible no promises thing on ice for an hour or two that afternoon.

Was this really the best time to contemplate violating him? Hell, when he was this close, some part of her was always considering violating him.

After answers from Ackley, she'd show Breck her gratitude.

"Who did you speak to?" she asked, her hand relaxing but staying put. "Who agreed to testify?"

Maybe she wouldn't be so irrelevant if lobbying was an option.

"A powerful man with the means to protect himself," Ackley said. "A man eager to put this mistake in his past. He's willing to give details, facts, dates, evidence. He's a man with his own interests to protect, and he'll do that vehemently."

"Ricardo Whey," she said to Ackley's jolt of surprise. "He'll give you what you want in return for immunity. And you wouldn't want to upset such an influential man when you'll be looking to get reelected."

"Ricardo Whey," Porter said. "Of Whey Media Conglomerates? One of the richest most influential men in Hollywood?" That would be the man. "Why would he get involved with the Chicago Gambattos?" That was an easy answer. So easy Porter got it himself. "Money. He had to be making a fortune to take that risk."

"He's a man who believes in his own invulnerability," Breck said, knowing the man better than she did. "Which is likely why he agreed to testify."

If her sister, Trish, believed Zairn was rich and righteous enough to ensure her safety, it wasn't a leap that Ricardo Whey thought his own ability superior.

"We have a lot of ground to cover." Ackley linked his fingers on the table. "But this won't be a singular operation. Mr. Whey doesn't leave things to chance and wants a contingency."

Hmm, funny, who else said that recently?

"Whey wants Chicago to take him down."

If Whey had the ability to exert some power there, he may fulfill her wish, without even knowing it.

"We can get your father for money laundering, racketeering, conspiracy, many things…"

Porter's forearms landed on the table. "Murder." The crown jewel of crimes, and one that could carry a hefty sentence. "Whey can give us Gambatto for murder."

"Multiple. We will prosecute him for his crimes here in Los Angeles. And we'll prosecute his son for murder." Except both men, as far as she was aware, were in Chicago. "This will need to be a joint operation. For both of us to get what we want."

"We can work something out," Porter said. "But you'll have to give me something first. Something to show the strength of the case. We've been trying to nail Gambatto Senior for years. We can't go all in until we know it's airtight. The minute we go to him, or he gets a whiff this is heading at him—"

"That won't happen," Ackley asserted. "This has to be kept close."

"Works for me, but what about your office?" Porter was right to be wary. "As soon as your people figure out there's a plan…"

"Compared to Chicago, there are fewer people here with an allegiance to him."

"And I've got this far without details being leaked," Porter defended his position. "This is important. Vitally important. This isn't just a crime for us. The Gambattos have wreaked havoc on Chicago for generations. Getting this man off the street and out of his position of power—"

"Preaching to me is pointless," Ackley said. "You know as well as I do that the power balance of your city has shifted, profoundly, in light of recent events. This is not a golden ticket, it won't solve all your problems."

"It will make a difference, a massive difference. And don't talk about my city as if yours is pristine. This happened on your watch too. Gambattos imported crime to your city and you sat by while it happened. Either you turned a blind eye or were oblivious to it happening. Neither says much about your intuition or ability."

Whoa, check the balls on that guy. Impressive. Ackley blustered as he argued back. Porter didn't shy from defending those in his city fighting the good fight.

"Enough," Breck silenced both men only a fraction of a second before she expected them to rise and take things up a notch. "You have jobs to do, and those jobs, for now, complement each other. If you start tearing each other apart, this fragile trust may be shattered."

"Let's just show each other a little professional courtesy."

"You don't have to be here for this," Ackley said, still amped by adrenaline.

Breck wasn't giving an inch. "I think we've proved you do."

Yes, she and Breck could leave and allow the prosecutors to put together a case they could both agree on. It wasn't necessary for her and Breck to be privy to it. That said, after the recent show, they may need a mediator. There was also a chance she could explain how one part related to another. Even without firsthand knowledge of current goings-on, she grew up with it and knew how it worked. They may need a Gambatto brain to think Gambatto.

The more she could do to take down the patriarch responsible for so much hurt, the better. And if she could hear their case, maybe she could garner some confidence in it, see how impossible it might be for her father to wriggle out of a lengthy sentence.

"My father is known for setting people against each other. Letting them do his work with just a few choice plays to detonate a conflict. Don't let him have the same satisfaction here. He's the enemy."

"Ricardo Whey," Breck said, stepping in to bring them back to the relevant point. "What exactly did he give you?"

A man not known for his scruples, Whey was notorious at looking out for himself. His own interest. Selfishly. No wonder he and her father got along. Still, there was a chance that by the end of this, she'd owe him a lot. Grievances aside, his aim matched hers. Did she really care if he got off scot-free? He was nothing to her and could deliver her the future she craved.

TWENTY-NINE

THEY SPENT MOST of the day secreted in that room with the prosecutors. Turned out her presence was useful, she educated them on the man, and maybe pressed a few of the lawyers' buttons to reiterate allowing her father to win was not an option.

Breck's fingers slid between hers after they left the conference room to descend to the elevator mezzanine. Her head was spinning and yet completely empty. Accepting that this was real, that the progress was considerable, would take some time.

A few feet from the elevators, Breck stopped to move in front of her. "How do you feel?"

Trust him to ask the only question she couldn't answer in that second, not with any level of diligence.

"It's like Christmas," she said, trying her best to be articulate. "When you're a kid, you know? There's all this anticipation. You picture what it will be, the excitement…"

"And it never lives up to expectation."

"It's tough to take in. I suppose I don't want to believe."

"Because you fear being disappointed."

"How often in life do the truly awful people get their comeuppance? Not often."

With a feather's touch, his fingers drifted across her cheek and over her hair. "It doesn't matter how long this takes. We'll keep going as long as necessary." Even knowing it was a given, she still appreciated him verbalizing his support. "This is a massive move in the right direction. You can start to let yourself believe."

"That we can be together." Sinking against him, the muscles of her neck relaxed. "You know that's the only reason I'm doing this, because I'm selfish, and I want you all to myself."

Her smile preceded a whisper of a laugh passing his lips. "You've had me all to yourself for years."

Because even when they weren't together, nothing else stuck. She wasn't sure he'd been intimate with anyone other than her for a long time. As much as she'd like to hear he hadn't, asking meant being prepared for the opposite answer. And she wasn't prepared, hence why she'd never ask.

"All this effort..." With a tilt of her head, her sassing eyes slunk to the right. "I do all of this for you and you blow it at the last hurdle."

"Blow it, huh?"

"Sure. The father of my children can't be a deadbeat. What do you take me for?"

"Ah, is that what I am?" His arms closed around her, yanking her tight to him. "You're thinking I should secure employment before impregnating you?"

"Would be the polite thing to do. And..." Drawing out the word, her fingers ascended his chest. "I happen to know of an open position."

"Do you?"

She might be teasing in one sense; in another, she was completely serious. Clearing her smile, she wanted to ensure he got that.

"Call your dad."

"Breckenridge will always be there."

"And you should always be with it. Your brothers need you."

"So will my wife and children." Discernment crossed his brows as he scrutinized her. "Are we talking about this? Planning our future?"

"If my father goes to jail…"

"Ricardo Whey will make sure of that. This is his cause too now the truth is emerging. If your father doesn't go down, Whey will, and he won't let that happen." And she'd get there. When the situation sank in. "You should talk to Tripp."

"He'll know plenty we don't," she muttered.

"He will, not that we should expect him to break any confidences."

That went without saying; they didn't call Tripp "Priest" for nothing.

"Do we have…?"

"What?"

"Is there any reason Whey would want to hurt us?"

"Personally? Not that I'm aware of. Mom knows more about the family." Yeah, because she was from the same streets. Though that made her sound ghetto, which couldn't be further from the truth. "Hey…" His curled fingers elevated her chin. "We've done nothing wrong."

Yet she couldn't shake the bad vibe. "I should be grateful; Whey's helping get us where we want to be."

"Talk to Tripp. If there's something we should know, he'll find a way to tell us." One way or another, he'd agree or disagree with her uncertainty. "Where would you like to eat tonight? In the suite or out somewhere?"

"Are you asking me out?"

"It's Valentine's Day."

That may be. Her mind had been elsewhere. "I thought you were poor."

"So I'll get you a slice of pizza."

Her cheeks plumped. "Everyone's sick of me and pizza."

Bowing, he touched his lips to hers. "Not me."

"I'll date you tonight because it's Valentine's Day, but tomorrow we're going back to New York."

"I thought we were staying until after the wedding."

She shook her head. "I can't be in LA that long."

"I have fifteen brothers. One of them will pick up the slack at the office."

"Some of them are still in school and one of them is here." Playing, she narrowed her eyes. "Are you telling me I'm replaceable?"

"No."

"That your brothers, that males, are better than females?"

"Definitely didn't say that. If you want to go back to New York, we'll leave right now. Why wait?"

And she may jump at that suggestion, except... "Roxie knows a fertility doctor here. One she trusts."

"A fertility doctor? Are we there yet?"

"Are we going to be parents tomorrow? No. And I am not conceding that our future is guaranteed, but we're here anyway, and Roxie's word is good. Why not?"

"Whatever you want, baby. Do we need an appointment?"

"Roxie said she'd call."

"If you knew about this, why didn't you tell me to come to LA?"

"I hadn't decided I was going to do anything about it yet. Everything's probably fine. Like I said, Roxie and I were talking, it came up and... I thought I might get checked out."

"Just you?"

"Well, you're here now. It wouldn't hurt to have some support."

"I'll be there."

"It's such a shame you're poor now," she said, splaying her hands on his body.

"Because this doctor costs money?"

She could cover that. There were levels between billionaire and destitute. Her job easily kept her afloat.

"Because the nurse accepts bribes."

"To what? Doctor the results?"

Wouldn't that be counterintuitive?

"No, to look the other way when a woman might want to join her man… to help obtain his… sample."

And that quickly changed his tune. "I'll find the money."

She laughed. "I want to get changed. If Tripp's in, and awake, we can ask him about Whey."

Putting an arm around her shoulders, he guided her toward the elevator. "Mom will know more about historical situations. Carolyn would be useful in relaying his current positions."

"Do you really want to involve them?" They stepped into the elevator and selected their floor. "The more people who know, the more complicated it could get further down the line."

The boundary between trust and protection was thin. Of course she trusted the Breckenridges, and Carolyn Hunt, but they were happy, spending time together, having fun. This wasn't the time for drama and negativity.

In the suite's living room, they found Tripp standing insanely close, like intimately close, to a woman she'd never seen before.

"Should've put a sock on the doorknob," Breck

said as his brother backed off.

"Ha, ha, very funny."

"We'll…" the woman said with hope and insecurity in equal measure.

"Yeah, you got it."

Tripp kissed the woman's head and she shuffled past them, meek smile on her face.

"You didn't have to do that," she said. "We'd have made ourselves scarce, we're going out anyway."

"No, it's no big deal," Tripp said, dropping onto the sofa. "Coming to the club tonight?"

"Mom and Carolyn—"

"Still shopping, or having cocktails, I don't know. You know what they're like when they get together."

"What did you get up to today?"

"Haven't got myself out of here yet."

Huh, so where did the woman come from? Was she left over from last night or someone Tripp had on call?

"I'm not surprised," Breck said. "Bet you didn't long wake up."

Half a smile and a shrug were Tripp's answer.

"Where did the woman come from?" she asked, still impressed by just how magnetic he could be. "How do you pick up a woman without leaving the suite?"

"Tripp never reveals his secrets." Breck went to block his brother's view of the TV just as Tripp picked up the remote. "What do you know about Ricardo Whey?"

"That wasn't subtle," she said, fighting to strengthen her jaw. "You ask just like that?"

"It's Tripp."

And they trusted Tripp.

Sighing, she sat beside him. "Okay, what do you know about Ricardo Whey?"

"Lots of stuff."

"I know things about Ricardo Whey," Roxie said, joining them. Oops, it hadn't occurred to her that anyone may be within earshot. "Why do you want to know?"

"You know things you can't tell anyone, Rox Out," Tripp said. "You know the rules."

"The frustrating rules."

It didn't help that people knew things if they couldn't share them.

"Is he trustworthy?" Breck asked. "When it comes to crunch time?"

Roxie examined her nails. "Ask his wife."

Okay, that was telling without telling. So he was a philanderer, that didn't mean he'd flake on them at the last minute. He couldn't anyway. If he didn't see through his side of the deal, Ackley would have no choice except to prosecute him. That would look good on a resume, a juicy scandal to feed the press at reelection time. Look at him, unafraid to go after power... Except that power may be exactly what stopped him from doing what was necessary.

"Does Whey have friends who can hurt us?" she asked because they had to know which direction to keep an eye on.

"Yes," Tripp said.

Roxie's smile spread. "But they won't..." And the beat that followed felt like a lifetime. "Because you have friends who can hurt him more. Hurt him personally, and in the wallet, which he really cares about."

"Rox Out..." Tripp's tone of warning deepened her curiosity. "If you're going to talk—"

"I don't need to talk. I won't say a word." In innocence, the woman showed both palms in surrender. "If it becomes necessary, they should know, we have their backs."

"Of course we do, but you have to check your pocket before making promises others will have to keep."

"If it comes to it, they'll do what's right. You can't honestly want him to screw over your family."

Not that this helped much when they couldn't leverage whatever their friends had without knowing it.

"I'd never let that happen," Tripp said. "But that's my deal. You don't have to get involved."

"When it comes to people I love..." Roxie asserted, "I get involved, every time."

"How do we use this?" Breck asked, proving himself one step ahead. "You can't reveal what you know."

"Just remind him that your brother has powerful friends. Some hold certain cards that Whey would rather the world didn't see."

"Won't he just counter that he'll hurt us back?" she asked. "The Breckenridges have powerful friends, yes, but so does Ricardo Whey."

Lowering her volume, Roxie leaned in. "I have a very big microphone and I'm not afraid to use it... or share it. If you want him broken, we can break him. Nothing he might have on us comes close, none of us. We can bring down his whole world."

And there was just enough of a thread of glee in that statement, would Roxie relish the chance?

"Excuse Rox," Tripp said, slouching and hooking his hands over the back of the couch. "The drama gets her off."

Then she was with the right man, and surrounded by the right circle of friends.

"We don't want to hurt him, not now."

"At the present time, his interests serve our cause," Breck said, resting a hand on her lower back. "If that should change..."

"We can mobilize in a snap."

"What about Ackley?"

"Oh, him I'd ruin in a heartbeat." Roxie didn't blink. "I may not even wait to be told."

"It's probably not in your interest to let Whey know you're close with Roxie," Tripp said. "Not while he's playing nice."

Close with Roxie? Was she? Shit, they'd known each other a matter of days and had already shared a pregnancy scare and the incrimination of a felon. Duration sort of didn't count in this scenario.

She nodded. "Okay."

"We're going out to eat," Breck said. "Would you like to join us?"

Exhaling, Tripp boosted himself up off the couch, swinging his arms at his sides. "Guess that's your way of asking me to foot the bill." He strolled over to pat his brother's shoulder. "Never thought I'd see the day, man."

"This isn't the day," she said, glancing at Tripp before becoming intent on Breck. "Because he's going back to Breckenridge."

"That was a short stint."

"Coy—"

"I mean it, Stat. This is important to me."

And his point was taken. He'd give up anything for her, she got it, but this was a step too far. He wanted to be there for her? Well, this was her way of being there for him. They were a family and needed to stick together.

THIRTY

THE NEXT DAY, Roxie made a call to the fertility clinic, and they got out of the suite without encountering the mothers, who were on their way for lunch. She and Breck wouldn't be missing much, wedding talk was the topic du jour. God, marriage, she couldn't even think about that.

The fertility clinic maybe wouldn't be the best of fun. Any experience that included a pelvic couldn't really be put under that banner. Luckily, paperwork and samples were all that had been demanded of them so far. Yeah, it was delaying the inevitable, but she wasn't sorry Breck's contribution could be done before the doc was ready for her. Sure worked out for Breck; the doc's delay gave them an opportunity to get cozy for a good cause. Opportunity or excuse?

Semantics.

"I really shouldn't…" the nurse by the admin desk said under her breath, gaze slinking left and right. "We have strict rules."

That they'd turned a blind eye too, at least once.

Though that previous time, Zairn Lomond was the one doing the charming. Which he kind of did professionally. His charisma was world-renowned. God love her wonderful Breck for all his virtues, but, unfortunately, he couldn't claim to have the same skill.

"No one has to know you made an exception."

Except Roxie, because she'd ask.

The phone on the desk rang, interrupting their negotiation. Given their lofty roles at Breckenridge, it would be mighty embarrassing if they failed to succeed on this one.

"I have to get that." The employee turned on her heels. "Give me a second."

Was that their cue to sneak on past? Maybe, if the woman had directed them to the location of an appropriate room. This was not a place someone wanted to start opening doors to check what was on the other side. Rather who was on the other side and what they might be doing.

Yep. That.

Shudder.

She tipped her head back to rest it on Breck. "How bad do you want it, baby?"

"We can always bring the cup back later."

"And I thought a guy like you might class up my life."

"Sorry to disappoint."

"Oh, Stat, you don't know how to do that."

The nurse finished the call and came back, something tugging on the corner of her lips. "The doctor needs to see you, Ms. Drury. Down the corridor, room three."

"Guess you're on your own, Stat," she said. "Enjoy."

Better that the doctor call her in before she tangle herself up in any compromising situations. Interruptions halfway through might be… inconvenient.

Breck reached for the cup on the counter, but the nurse swiped it out of the way. "That may not be necessary."

Oh, shit, what did that mean? Could they really tell from blood and urine that a person was completely infertile? That was a damn quick turnaround; they couldn't have handed over those samples more than twenty minutes ago. Though if this was the kind of place people like Zairn Lomond used, they had to be dealing with the elite. Could be their facilities were that swift.

Taking Breck's hand, she was ready to face whatever might happen in that room. "If you're not needed here, you're coming with me."

"Uh, you may want to go in alone," the nurse said. "It's recommended."

"Recommended that I don't take the man I intended to father my children into a fertility meeting with a doctor?" Did that mean it was really bad? "What can he say to me that I wouldn't want Breck to hear?"

"It's okay." Breck kissed her head. "I'll wait here."

Except she didn't want him to wait there. It could only be bad news. They couldn't have a judgment on Breck's sperm when they didn't have it yet. It could only be her.

"What if I'm sick," she said, wide eyes locking on his. "I could have cancer or something else horrific."

His hand tightened around hers. "Room three?"

"We don't test for that." The nurse was missing the point. This could be profound news. If she needed support, there was only one person she wanted with her. "It's something we suggest to all women in this situation."

All women? This kind of thing had to happen a lot.

"A suggestion isn't mandatory," her guy asserted.

Tugging her from the spot, Breck strode down the hallway so fast, she almost lost her footing. Trust him to react with such purpose. No one would keep him from her, not when she might need him.

It helped that she couldn't think of anything she wouldn't share. Whether sick or infertile, she wouldn't conceal that news from him. Wouldn't? Maybe she should, to protect him from it. Trouble was, if she came out of that room telling Breck they were over for good and tried to put distance between their lives—because she'd secretly discovered being terminal—he'd read her in a nanosecond.

"Wait…" She pulled him to a halt. "What if it is bad news?"

"We'll deal with it. You'll get the best medical care in the world. It's insulting you'd make me say that."

Yeah, but that wasn't her point. "No, what if it's bad news like I can't have children?"

"You'll be disappointed, and I'll work through that with you, whatever you need, but it changes nothing."

"It changes everything. I want you to live a full and happy life, if I'm incapable of giving that to you—"

"There are options beyond our basic biology; something you know. Regardless of what happens in that room, your wishes are clear. You want children, so we'll have children, one way or another. Do you believe we'd love them any less if we went for fertility treatment or the adoption route?"

No. Breck's ability to love was in no doubt; his whole family was the same.

"I don't deserve you," she said with a sigh and a smile. "You're the most incredible man that I could ever…"

"This is not a grand act that deserves praise."

Him being his usually humphing self, so straightforward. "It's not complicated. There's nothing any doctor could say that would change our path."

And she might argue with that, except she'd feel exactly the same way in his position. "It's better to know now."

"Yes, so we can make decisions."

"Together."

"Always together."

He really was something else. "How do you still manage to surprise and humble me after all these years?"

"It's a gift." His knuckles skimmed her cheek. "No more delays."

That wasn't her intention, though it hadn't not been her intention either. Could've been her subconscious' intention. Science was science, no matter how she tried to postpone it.

Breck knocked once but went inside without waiting for a response.

The doctor rose from the desk, a smile on his face, though it faltered a little when he glanced from Breck to her and back.

"I'm going to guess he's glaring," she said, too busy trying to read the doctor to check Breck's expression. "It's his default, he doesn't mean it."

Whatever was wrong, it wasn't the doctor's fault. Was it hers? She tried to eat right. Didn't smoke. Didn't drink that much either. Wouldn't it be hilarious to find out the cause of her issue was genetic? How much more could her family take from her?

"We recommend—"

"We know what you recommend." Yep, Breck was in no nonsense mode, no way of getting around him when he was so determined. "If you want me to leave the room, you better bring an army."

Oh, shiver. Prioritizing her needs was his default

too, and even after all this time, it still made her swoon.

"It's okay." She led Breck to the chairs opposite the doctor's desk and kept hold of his hand even when they descended into them. "I want him here. You can talk freely."

"Okay." The doctor sat and an age passed before he spoke again. "We have to perform another procedure."

Yes, she'd known that more than bodily fluids would be required of her. "Procedure?"

"An ultrasound."

Again, expected. "To check my ovaries?"

No wonder they didn't need Breck, his proximity wouldn't change the outcome.

"To check your fetus."

"To check my…" He may as well have slapped her across the face. "Wait, my what?"

His smile grew. "You're pregnant."

"No, I'm not," she said, adamant. "I did a test."

"They're not always accurate, which is why we'd like to do the ultrasound."

"You think the test I did was a false negative?"

"It's possible."

"How do you know your test wasn't a false positive?"

"We'll confirm with the ultrasound, if you consent to proceed."

They'd come there to check whether biological children were an option for them, it would be ridiculous to withdraw her consent at that moment.

"Yes, but I… You want to do an ultrasound to find out if I'm pregnant…" That made sense. Something else didn't. "Why would you suggest the father of that child not be present?"

"In case I'm not the father of the child," Breck answered.

Oh.

The poor doctor squirmed. "We often find it's best to give the news to the mother first. With the ultrasound, we can narrow down the date of conception."

Right, was their "suggestion" something they reserved for all women or only the unmarried ones?

Standing up, pushing her shoulders back, she didn't want to get her hopes up before they were certain, a hundred percent certain.

"Let's do this."

She didn't need a gown or to do anything other than roll up her top and down the waistband of her pants. And then it was there. After all the waiting, she didn't need to be told what the sound was when the doctor turned up the volume and adjusted the monitor so they could both see.

"Yes, you are definitely pregnant. Strong heartbeat. Steady." Yeah. Wow. Breck's hand was already in hers; the physical link strengthened them and right now, they both needed that. "Around twelve weeks."

Hold on just a second... "Twelve? No, that can't be right. That's November and I didn't—"

"Conception may have been around the first week of December."

Because they counted from her last period rather than the intercourse date, right. "Okay, but that doesn't make sense either, because we didn't—"

"I don't care," Breck said, kissing the back of her hand locked in his. "This baby is our future."

No matter who the father was? Was that what he meant? Sweet or insulting? Anger was so far beyond her capability right then.

"Way to call me a slut in front of the doctor, Stat," she said, too giddy and confused to do anything other than exhale a laugh. "If there's a baby in there, you put it in there. No question. I haven't been with any man but you since..." Did her memory go that far back? "More years than I want to admit. We weren't together in December, not at the..."

Oh...

"The Simion deal?"

"That doesn't count," she dismissed him, "that was at work. Work doesn't count, we always say that."

Because in Breckenridge HQ, there were highs and lows, adrenaline and grievance. Emotions could shift like a riptide and sometimes they needed to... vent those emotions. Work was a, "Yeah, we did it, but we're not going to talk about it," venue. Sometimes they did or they didn't, it was all allowed because it didn't count.

The doctor laughed. "If there was sexual contact..."

Oh, there had been that. "But we... That means I was pregnant at New Year's when we..."

She hadn't even asked him about having kids at that point. Not seriously. Not in an active way like she had at New Year's. And, shit, that meant she'd spent a million dollars for no reason. Other than the charity.

"Would you like a video?" the doctor asked.

"Yes," she said quickly, then landed her certainty on Breck. "We are not telling your mom."

"She'll be ecstatic."

"There are options..." The doctor's tone dropped to a serious octave. "If you don't want this child—"

"We want him," Breck said, "or her. My mother is..."

"Full on," she added, not ready for the rocket to hit the stratosphere. "We have to get used to this news first."

Pregnant. Just like she'd wanted. Phew. Deep breath. With her father and the case, could she be pregnant right now? With Breck's baby? This little one had kind of stolen their choice. Decisions had to be made now, there was a clock. And she'd thought the last few days were a mental and emotional rollercoaster? Child's play. Nothing to this psychological slalom.

The paternity of the baby, when she'd decided to go for it, was supposed to be a secret.

This wasn't a secret.

She was having Breck's baby.

THIRTY-ONE

HE FIXATED ON her stomach a lot. Too much for someone who was supposed to be keeping a secret.

"You keep looking at me like that, the whole world is going to know."

Even sitting side-by-side, facing the front of the plane, she could tell he was staring again.

Breck was the kind of guy who took everything in stride. He was never overwhelmed or intimidated, he was a planner. And this most definitely hadn't been the plan.

"No one here knows who we are. It's a commercial flight."

Shifting her head in the leather headrest, she got closer, but didn't actually meet his eye. "When was the last time you flew commercial?"

"Bastian owns an airline."

"I know he does, that's why I asked."

"If you'd let me call—"

"I want to be home, okay?" That's what she said the moment they hit the sidewalk in LA. They'd gone straight to the airport. "I don't want to wait. You could've stayed in LA if you wanted."

"I can't see myself leaving your side any time soon."

"We're glued together?" That wouldn't be subtle either. "Won't that be fun?"

They were flying commercial, yes. In first class, not slumming it in economy. It may be unusual, but it wasn't any hardship. Luxury, when within reach, found a way.

The preened flight attendant approached wearing a broad plastic grin. "Can I get you anything? Food? Something to drink?"

Returning the expression, she didn't envy the woman her job. "No, thank you."

"You can bring her—"

"I don't want anything, thank you," she said, cutting Breck off. After the woman continued up the aisle, she flashed him a glare. "Have I ever needed you to speak for me in the past?"

"I'm speaking for my child."

"Start that and you'll be far, far away from this pregnancy. I'll change the locks, hire security to maintain a perimeter."

Okay, maybe she wouldn't go that far, but she was making a point.

Like it bounced off, he became more discerning. "We need a bigger apartment."

Maybe the perimeter thing wasn't such a bad idea after all. "Oh, *we* do? Do *we*?"

"Unless you want to move into B House." Ha, what a comedian. "We'd never have to worry about childcare."

She laughed. "Or see our child again."

"I'll talk to Mom, she won't overstep."

Alice would, but it would be welcome. The

woman had so much child rearing experience she could run her own university. Keeping the news quiet at that juncture was about rebounding from shock, not because she thought the Breckenridges would react negatively.

How quickly things changed. At that time the previous week, the idea they'd even considered having a child was a secret. That she'd been considering it, Breck wasn't supposed to be attached to the notion at all.

"We shouldn't be talking about this. You're supposed to be the sperm donor."

There was that deadpan look again. "Coy."

"I know. Okay? I know. You want to be involved."

"I am involved. We will raise this child together. You're out of excuses. We've put things to bed with your father."

"Not yet. We can't afford to get complacent. That's usually exactly when he sneaks past and gets his way."

"We cannot live our lives in fear."

Uh, which was exactly her point all along.

"Once he's in prison—"

"Chances are you'll have given birth by then. He's under bail restrictions in Chicago at the moment. Soon they'll bring additional charges and he'll be unable to reach us." In an ideal world. He gathered her hand into his, using his other to tempt her jaw around until they were looking into each other. "What's really holding you back?"

"You don't have a job." The tilt of his head emptied her lungs. "I don't know. I want this; I know I want this."

"And some part of you thinks you don't deserve it?"

Was that it? Once again he proved he might truly know her better than she knew herself. That conclusion wasn't even—look at her life, her history, her genetics. Was it right to...? But it was done. Their child existed.

Her own fingers trailed to her belly. "Can we just go home, get some sleep, and try to make sense of this tomorrow?"

When maybe sense might be in order again. She'd woken up wanting to become a mother, ready to find out if it was a possibility for her future. Instead, she'd learned motherhood was already upon her.

Breck was right, they needed a bigger apartment.

THIRTY-TWO

SHE LEFT THE APARTMENT that morning, after a good night's sleep, while Breck was in the shower. It wasn't an act of cowardice, it was a desperate grab for normality. That was the first day that week she'd got up and gone into Breckenridge as was her usual routine.

No lawyers. No District Attorneys, or Assistant District Attorneys. No evidence. No testifying. No Gambattos or crime lords. Just work. Good, normal, any-other-day work.

That was the idea anyway.

Pregnancy was such a huge thing. It didn't help that no one else knew. No one except Breck, who was doing exactly what she needed him to do by not calling or tracking her down. As much as she needed him, she needed space, and he got that.

Did he have to be so damn wonderful all the time?

Work might be getting done, but her heart wasn't in it. There was a child growing in her belly. A real baby. Some moments she got a zip of excitement. Others were dread. What parental role model did she have to emulate? None.

Maybe it would be better for the kid if she handed him over to Breck and ran a million miles. Gambatto selfishness might creep in otherwise. What if it didn't work out the way she thought. The baby could be born and maybe she wouldn't be flooded with the love parents were supposed to feel.

Would she resent the child, as her parents resented her, and anyone else who didn't subscribe to their way of life? She could corrupt him. What had she been thinking continuing the Gambatto line?

"How was LA?"

Benedict Breckenridge. Family patriarch. CEO. Mentor. Philanthropist. One of the most successful men of his generation. Yep, that was Benedict Breckenridge standing in her doorway.

"Breck called you?"

That kind of came across as an accusation, which was so not her intention.

His genuine smile warmed the room, activating her trust. "Not today," he said, strolling further inside. "You didn't come to say hello."

And if she'd been on vacation, that might be something she'd do. They didn't talk all the time, they weren't best buds, but there probably wasn't a person on earth she trusted more.

"I'm pregnant."

The strained words burst out. She spat them across the room; the ache of whatever emotion she battled came out in a cough like a confession that burdened her soul. This guy had to have magical powers.

He stepped back, reaching behind himself to close the door without looking.

"Congratulations."

She waited. And waited.

Well, if he wasn't going to say anything… "I thought that I wanted to be a mother, but now it's really happening…"

"It's overwhelming. Don't be afraid, we all go through it. When did you find out?"

"Yesterday."

He gestured at the couch by the window and headed that way. Quick to jump up, she followed and sat while he poured water from the pitcher on the side table.

"The news has barely had a chance to sink in yet." He handed her the glass and sat in the corner of the couch, one arm along the back, the other on the arm. "Give yourself some time. Is that why you left LA?"

She sipped, their eyes locked, until she had to concede with a shrug and lower the glass. "Maybe."

"Because Alice was there."

That was a truth she had come to grips with. "Alice would've taken one look at me and I'd have cried. She doesn't need me crying all over her. The woman has sixteen sons to worry about."

"She can worry about them and her daughter at the same time. Though this isn't a worry, this is a celebration. You'll be a wonderful mother."

If only she had that confidence. "Are you so sure about that?" The glass went to her knee. "I'm a Gambatto."

"You're a Breckenridge. I've seen how you love and I don't doubt you have plenty of it to lavish on your offspring."

After another sip, it wasn't so easy to meet his gaze. "Are you going to ask me?"

"Ask you what? Are you happy?"

Her eyes went to his. "Who the father is."

Another smile. "I don't need to ask. Breck will love this child, fiercely, whether it carries his DNA or not. We all will."

Even after all these years, the family still astounded her with their acceptance.

"It is. Breck's. He is the father, and he knows, I... I asked him not to tell people. To keep this between us until we'd processed it."

"He'll support whatever you need."

"I don't want you to think I kept it a secret, or that he did. We're not ashamed, I... I just don't know what will come next."

"This is your journey. You decide what comes next. Together."

"Should we get married?"

Guidance from her mentor would be greatly appreciated and eagerly accepted. Sometimes it was easier just to have someone give out instructions to be followed. And this was Ben, she'd follow his instructions without hesitation.

"Do you want to get married?"

"He hasn't asked me."

Ben's laugh was a surprise. "Because he knows you better than that. He would never blurt out the question without forethought. At the slightest hint of obligation, you'd shut him down. You want to get married for love, the same as he does."

"He's asked me before... not recently with everything, but... we did talk about it."

"And your concerns about your family always held you back. From what I understand, that's being cleaned up."

"I had to do something. Breck left here, Breckenridge, to put distance between him and... what worried me. He did it for us and I couldn't be the reason he... he loves his family."

"And we will continue to love him regardless of where he works, lives, whether he gets married or doesn't. Alice always said you were his only chance at it."

"A normal life?"

"True happiness."

"Was she high at the time?"

The depth of appreciation in his low laugh offered relief. "Marrying for love. Soulmates do exist, so Alice tells me. Given my own experience, I have no evidence to the contrary. If my eldest wants to be happy, he has to spend his life with his soulmate. Marriage doesn't matter. Who we're biologically related to, none of it is as important as love and respect."

"Support not judgment," she whispered and twisted to put the glass on the table behind her. "I want to spend my life with him."

"I guarantee he feels the same."

"He's told me as much."

"So be together, what's the problem?"

That niggling doubt wouldn't go away. "What if my family broke me too much? What if I can't be fixed and rounded and...? It's so much. Last week, I was barely thinking about this and now we're... I want to be with him; I'm having his baby. He's literally the father of my future."

God, when she put it like that...

"Your family didn't break you. They may have tried, but you walked away. At a young age too, that was how confident you were that you didn't want the future your parents envisioned. You're strong, Sequoia, don't doubt yourself."

"Would you take him back here? Breck?"

"That goes without saying."

Yes, it did. Fired by the certainty of a man she respected so much, the possibilities began to align.

"This child will be a part of all of our lives."

"Yes. A welcome addition."

Not just a part of their lives, the little one would be spoiled as the first of the next generation.

"I need to talk to Breck." In person. As soon as possible. She shifted to the edge of the seat and paused. "You're going to tell Alice even if I ask you not to tell her, aren't you?"

"I keep nothing from my wife," he said. "But this is news better received from you and Breck." He leaned in to kiss her cheek and murmured, "Just tell her soon."

Because he wouldn't want to keep anything from her, and maybe didn't trust himself not to follow her example and blurt it out.

The first place she'd check was their apartment. If Breck wasn't there, she could at least change before tracking him down. Where else would he be? Not Crimson without his brother there. Darroch's, maybe, or B House. At a job interview? He could be literally anywhere and she didn't want to call. He'd worry if she sounded amped, and right then, she probably did.

One step at a time.

THIRTY-THREE

BEFORE SHE TURNED the key in her apartment lock, she could smell it: paint. Someone on their floor must be decorating. It was a fleeting thought until on going inside, its concentration assaulted her. Not some neighbor. No, someone was painting in her apartment. She rounded into the hallway and was drawn to the second bedroom with its wide open door and pure white walls. Uh... those walls had been red when she left.

The floor was covered and next to a ladder she didn't know they had, Breck stood, roller in hand. Her mouth opened, sure, because she should say something... but she was just confused.

"Why did...?"

"It's the nursery," he said, putting the roller down. "You shouldn't be in here."

"The nursery? And you thought it should be white?"

"I thought we should have a fresh start." Putting an arm around her, he directed her out of that room and into their bedroom. "I didn't know how you felt about colors, if you preferred a mural or paper. This is a blank canvas, ready for whatever you decide." He frowned. "This is early for you. What happened? Why are you home at this time?"

"Nothing happened, I just..." Could she get away with saying she missed him? "We have to tell your mom."

"Okay."

"With some urgency."

"Why? Is something wrong?"

Was this going to be the pattern throughout her pregnancy? Better that he cared enough to be concerned than the opposite.

"Nothing's wrong..." Truth time. "I told your dad." With a wince, she braced. "I'm sorry. I didn't mean to, it came out all on its own."

He relaxed. "Don't worry. You're close. I assume he agreed not to tell Mom."

"I don't want him to have to lie."

"Sure, we can—"

"Wait..." She caught his arm as he started to pass. "I'm not done. We should... talk."

"Because people will ask questions. Dad wouldn't—"

"He didn't. Support, not judgment. He didn't even ask me who the father was."

"Because he knows it makes no difference to our future."

Oh, so matter of fact. "Maybe I want to run away with the fictitious father."

"And you can, providing it's fictitious running away. You said you'd only been with me..."

"Would you actually doubt that?" she teased. "How many women have you been screwing around with between our trysts?"

"I won't grace that insult with an answer."

Other people didn't exist for them, not in a romantic context.

"We'll need a bigger apartment," she said.

"Not necessarily, we have two rooms here, that's enough."

"Do you really want to live at B House?"

"Where we live makes little difference."

"What about work?" she asked. "Your father says you can come back to Breckenridge."

"That's up to you."

Startled, her hands stopped mid-rise to his hips. "Up to me? You know how I feel about you at Breckenridge."

"Yes. You worry that your father will gain influence over me or my family's business interests and finances if he's still on the street." And technically he was, for the moment anyway. "I'm not convinced you'll feel any other way until after his sentence. Maybe it will drag on until after he appeals."

Which he would.

Seeing it from Breck's perspective, the waiting would stretch on forever. He'd wait. He'd said he'd wait. Their child would be born and he'd still wait.

Power. That was what her father craved and she was giving it all to him. He ran her life, would she let him ruin it too?

No. No more. She had to be stronger than she had been, stronger than her father. And there was her strength with her: Breck. He'd always been her strength. With him, she could get through anything. They only had to trust and decide to leap.

Instinct took her down, onto a knee, scaring him into a crouch. Only her smile stopped him.

"Rankin Breckenridge, my Stat, will you marry me?" That widened his eyes so much a whisper of a laugh escaped her. "I don't want to wait anymore. I don't want my father to feature so heavily in our lives." Before the last few days, they may not have spoken of him often, but he'd lingered, there in the background. "I want to get married, have our child—"

"And live happily ever after?"

Leaving her there on her knees, he went to the nightstand and opened the drawer.

"Is that it?" she asked, staying put. It would be ironic if just as she embraced the possibility of forever, he dismissed it. "You didn't answer me."

"No," he said, surprising her on his return when he kneeled down with her. Before she could ask what was going on, he popped open a box to show her a ring. "Because I want you to answer me."

"You have a ring?"

"It's my grandmother's." Of course it was because that was just like the Breckenridges to have a ring tradition. "I can't remember a time I didn't love you, Coy. In some ways we're so different, in others we're exactly the same. Whatever the future brings us, I want us to tackle and enjoy it together. Will you be my wife, Sequoia?"

Tears blurred her eyes when her lips curled. "Your speech was so much better than mine."

"I've had a lot of time to think about what I want to say." And she'd just hit on the idea to propose seconds ago. "There aren't enough words to express what I feel for you. I know I can't live without you. I'll do whatever you need me to do—"

Touching his lips, she silenced him. "I'll marry you." A teardrop skittered from her lashes. "I'll bear your children…" As he smiled, hers grew again. "But you're coming back to work with me tomorrow."

He laughed. "Okay. If you insist."

If she truly thought leaving Breckenridge made him happy, she'd support his leaving one hundred percent. Breckenridges were a rare breed, they genuinely cared about each other and liked spending time together. Whether he admitted it or not, Breck basked in his role of responsibility. He liked to have authority and valued his brothers' respect.

When his lips sank onto hers, every muscle relaxed. Pulling herself close, she wrapped her arms around his neck, holding on as he stood and scooped her up to carry her to the bed.

For all the times they'd ever made love, nothing could match the difference forever made. Taking him into her body had always been a delight, but this was more than fun. They connected, like the physical joining somehow united their souls and minds too. Maybe Alice was right, could be soulmates were a thing after all.

"We shouldn't find out the sex until the birth," she said, lying naked in his arms.

"Okay."

"And I want to work from home for a while. I don't want to miss the early days or give up my job."

"Whatever you want."

"Should I feed the baby myself?"

His lips buried themselves in her hair. "That decision is entirely yours. We know that breast is best, but that doesn't make it inevitable."

"Your mom breastfed."

"Some of us. Though she'd never tell us which ones. She'll be happy to talk to you about it, if you have questions."

"I have a feeling she and I will be discussing a lot in the near future." Her fingertips danced up his torso. "We should tell her."

"Want me to call?"

Shifting, she showed him a smile. "Probably a good idea to get dressed first. I want to see her reaction."

Which meant a video call.

"You know, baby, she'll be so ecstatic, I doubt she'd notice our clothes."

"Okay, we'll make the call," she said, stretching as she sat up. "After we get out of the shower."

With her hand in his, she led him into the bathroom. Life delivered, no one could deny that. Sometimes hardship, sometimes delight, it gave and it took away. So long as she had her guy and their family, they'd weather in rapture whatever came next.

Read more from the Roxiverse in *Nothing to The Wedding...*

Thank you for reading this tale!
If you can, please take the time to review.

~

Ask your local library for more Scarlett Finn
novels!

~

For all things Scarlett Finn
check out:

www.scarlettfinn.com

Next in the Roxiverse:

SCARLETT FINN